SPOTTER

BROTHERS COURAGEOUS, BOOK 3

VANESSA GRAY BARTAL

DRY CREEK PRESS

PROLOGUE

Three years ago…

She stood beside the register as if waiting for someone, looking out over the department store without seeing any of the clothes. Small, dark, and curvaceous, the first word that came to mind was *luscious*. Kelsey liked using that word when it came to women like her, women who were so curvy there was almost too much of them to love. Almost.

If he had a type, it would be tall stacked blonds because, more often than not, those were the women he usually dated. He didn't have a type, though, because he loved all women. Even ugly women; he really, really loved the female of the species. And they loved him. He knew he was nice looking and could be charming when he wanted to be. He had always had a way with the ladies, but since he became a marine it was like shooting fish in a barrel. *Oooh, you're a marine? Let's go somewhere and talk about it.* Ding! Magic words.

This woman intrigued him because, despite having a rocking physique and thick black hair that hung to the middle of her back, she looked like butter wouldn't melt in her mouth. That was something his grandmother used to say that meant a woman was cold. But how could someone look so passionate and cold at the same time?

He walked to the counter beside the woman and spoke to the employee behind the register. "How much?" he asked, loudly enough for short, dark, and curvy to hear.

"How much what, sir?" the employee asked, confused.

"How much for the life-size Latina Barbie doll?" he asked, pointing to the other woman.

The employee chuckled. "I guess you'll have to ask her," she said, turning her attention to the next person in line.

Kelsey moved over to stand in front of the woman he was trying to impress. She was smiling. Ding! "That's such an odd coincidence," she said. "I was going to ask how much for the life-size G.I. Joe, but then I realized it was full of horse manure." She took her eyes off him and looked over his shoulder, scanning the store again.

"What are you looking for?" he asked.

"My can of pepper spray. I'm sure I had it here a minute ago." She still wasn't looking at him, which was odd. Had she seen him? He was gorgeous, if he did say so himself.

He waved his hand in front of her face and she frowned at him. "I'm checking to make sure you're not blind. That would have been awkward if we stood here talking for a long time and then you whip out one of those special canes as you walk away and I realize you couldn't see me the whole time."

"Oh, I see you," she said. "Believe me, I see you."

Now it was his turn to frown because when she said it, it didn't sound like a good thing. "So you have a serious boyfriend or something? I'm not getting the married vibe from you."

"Why don't you think I'm married?" she asked.

"Because you look too good. Married women have that I've-got-my-man-so-I'm-giving-up look."

"That is not true," she said. "All of my friends are married, and none of them look like that."

Oh, so that was it. She was living in the land of bitterness. Perhaps she had been attached but it had ended badly. And now all her friends were married and she was jealous. Yikes, her type could be dangerous because they could quickly turn clingy and desperate. Still, she was presenting a challenge, and there was nothing Kelsey liked better than a challenge.

"All your friends are married, huh?" he asked, his tone sympathetic. "I bet that hurts. Maybe you haven't found Mr. Right yet."

She made a fist and pressed it to her forehead, squeezing her eyes shut as she took a deep breath. It was possible the action meant she was exasperated with him, but he couldn't be sure. Women didn't often get that look with him, the one that meant they really wanted to punch him but were refraining. "You know, you're right," she said, opening her eyes and forcing a smile. "I'm terribly sad and alone, but now that I've met you that's all going to change, Random Stranger. Truly, you are my every dream come true. When can we get married and have babies? Because everyone knows that what every single woman really desires is a husband and babies. I'm new to the area, so maybe you can recommend one of those quickie chapels or a judge who will take a bribe. Let's do this. Today. Go get a ring. I'm a size six; I'll wait here." She pointed to the ground as if to indicate she was rooted to the spot.

"Wouldn't you feel silly if I really did it?" he said.

"No, I wouldn't because the 'I'm crazy' vibe is strong with you. I'm running out of ways to tell you I'm not interested, so I'll try saying the words: I'm not interested."

Kelsey didn't believe her, but it was that same sort of persistence that had helped him survive boot camp and sniper school. He didn't quit, even when the odds were against him. "Okay, here's the deal. I'm here with a buddy, and he bet me fifty bucks I couldn't get the next woman I see to kiss me. So if you don't give in here and unbend a little, I'm going to be out fifty bucks."

He thought maybe she would laugh or refuse him so he could move on to another tactic. He didn't expect her to stand on her toes, cup his face in her hands, pull his mouth to hers, and kiss him. And not a friendly peck on the lips, but a deep soul kiss, one that had him responding without conscious thought because it was that good. His hand slid to her waist and gripped hard while her leg curled around his thigh. They were about three seconds from becoming indecent, but then she abruptly let him go and took a step back, still looking completely composed. Meanwhile he gawked at her, mouth agape, nearly undone. He was about to reach for her again, because how could he not after a kiss like that. But she spoke.

"There you go. Enjoy your money. Now leave me alone." This time she didn't wait for him to walk away. Instead, she turned and took a step away and then her phone rang. He watched, dazed, as she pulled it out and spoke. "Hey, *hermonito*. Where are you?" She stopped short and looked around the store again. "I'm in the men's department, and I don't see you. By the cash register. Okay, I'll keep waiting." She bit her lip, waiting, and then she smiled. "There. I see you." She closed the phone and tucked it in her pocket before rushing forward and throwing her arms around a little marine, and Kelsey's chagrin intensified because the woman was hugging his brand-new teammate. Had he hit on the little guy's girlfriend? Awkward, and also a breakage of cardinal rule number one: never go for a teammate's girl.

Lolly eventually let go of the woman and noticed Kelsey's silent inspection. "Oh, good, you're here, too. This is my sister, Mellisandra. Melly, this is my teammate and roommate, Kelsey Adams."

"Oh, great, life keeps getting better and better," Melly said, her tone full of sarcasm even though she politely extended her hand, waiting to shake.

Kelsey finally roused from his stupor and smiled. Life really did keep getting better and better. "What's with the outstretched hand? We're practically family now. Doesn't that entitle me to a hug? Maybe a kiss?" He opened his arms and waited.

"How about a lawsuit for sexual harassment?"

He dropped his arms and his smile. "You can't joke about stuff like that. I could get thrown out of the corps for dishonorable behavior."

"Who says I'm joking?" she said.

He wasn't sure. She was hard to read. "Lolly, is she joking?" he asked.

"Wait, what? What did you call him?" she asked, and there was no mistaking her anger this time.

"Lolly. That's his new name 'cause he represents the Lollypop Guild."

Her jaw dropped. Kelsey was delighted to see some emotion finally leak behind her cool exterior. "No, absolutely not. You cannot call him that. His name is Jesus."

Kelsey rolled his eyes. "I know his name. Everyone gets a nickname. It's part of the code." He scanned her up and down. "I'll call you Luscious."

It's possible she would have leapt on him then, but Lolly grabbed her around the waist and held her back. "Guys, guys, guys, let's all take a moment here and relax. We're going to be seeing a lot of each other. You're going to need to learn to get along," he said.

Melly did take a breath and even mustered a smile for her brother. "For your sake, I will try to get along with him."

They turned to Kelsey together, but he made no such promise. Arguing with her had been the most fun he'd had in ages. He could only hope there was much more to come. "Welcome to the family," he said, holding out his arms again. "How about that kiss?"

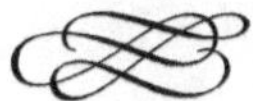

CHAPTER 1

Kelsey's alarm rang, and he was glad he had set it. He shouldn't have needed an alarm on this most momentous of days, but apparently he did because it went off for a solid two minutes before he woke enough to shut it off.

He sat up, letting his tongue try and work some moisture back into his mouth as he looked around for a beer. Using alcohol to try and cure a hangover was called the hair of the dog for good reason because Kelsey's mouth tasted exactly as if he had licked a dog. He found a few sips in a half-crushed can beside his bed and winced when he tipped his head back to drink. Ouch. Ouch for everything. His head, his joints, his face. Everything hurt. He was getting too old for this, and the irony was it was supposed to be Nick who was in this condition. How many times had they talked about getting wasted at their bachelor parties? Not many because they hadn't really believed they would be getting married before thirty, but whenever the topic had come up, they had definitely planned to party all night.

Instead what happened was Kelsey and the new guy, Travis, kept the party going, hopping from bar to bar, drinking whatever landed in front of them while Nick and Ashton probably drank a combined total of four sips of alcohol the entire night. What was up with them?

Since when did falling in love have to make you sober? Since when did it mean you couldn't have any fun? Although, Kelsey didn't feel very fun this morning. There was a good possibility he was going to puke all over everything as soon as he stood up.

Someone pounded on his door and they might as well have been pounding on his head. "Guh," Kelsey managed to groan and whoever was on the other side of the door must have taken it as a signal to enter because he pushed open the door and poked his head in.

"Time to hit the road, sleepyhead." It was Ashton, sounding so cheerful and wide awake Kelsey wanted to punch him if only he could get his arms to work. "Dude, you look terrible. You have like thirty seconds to shower before we have to leave. Let's go, man." He closed the door and walked back out again, oblivious to Kelsey's dark scowl.

He was really getting tired of Truck and Nick and their combined euphoria. So they were in love. Big deal. Kelsey could be in love if he wanted, but he didn't want. He was twenty seven, much too young to settle for anyone. His thoughts strayed to Melly, but he couldn't go there because thoughts of Melly inevitably led to thoughts of Lolly, and he couldn't think about the little marine who had died in his arms a few short months ago. Not yet. Not ever. So he mustered all the energy he could find, focusing it on his legs as he pulled himself to a standing position and staggered toward the bathroom where he puked up everything he had ever eaten. Thankfully he made it to the toilet and wouldn't have to clean up the floor or any other surface.

He flushed and reached into the shower, turning it on full blast so when he shrugged out of his clothes and stepped under the spray, it stung his skin like thousands of tiny needles. The sensation was more painful than refreshing, but it had the same effect of bringing some semblance of wakefulness to his foggy brain.

He could have stood there all day letting the water wash over him, letting it clean his stink and mental cobwebs. But he didn't because today wasn't about him, it was about his best friend, and, even though he didn't feel like it, Kelsey would have to paste on a smile and do his part as Nick's best man. So after a too short time under the hot water, he exited the shower and threw on some clothes, belatedly remembering to splash on cologne and slap some deodorant under his pits. Once he buttoned himself into the monkey suit, he was definitely going to need some deodorant.

Ashleigh's mother was in charge of making sure their uniforms were at the church on time, so Kelsey didn't have to remember that part, which was good because there's no way he would have. He grabbed his razor, intending to shave in the car, and found his three other roommates waiting on him, Nick and Ashton pacing impatiently back and forth.

Travis, the new guy, looked almost as good as they did and no worse the wear after their night of partying a few hours ago.

"Dude, what gives?" Kelsey asked. "What's your secret?"

"I'm younger than you, Grandpa," Travis said. His last name was Vega, giving him the automatic nickname of Vegas. Kelsey frowned at the back of his head as they exited the house. He was pretty sure he didn't like the kid. Had he ever been that cocky and arrogant? He was a stark contrast from Lolly's sweetness and reserve. They had forged a bond the previous night because they had been the only two bent on getting wasted, but now in the light of day Kelsey realized he didn't much care for the guy. Though, to be fair, he probably wouldn't have cared for anyone who tried to fill Lolly's shoes so soon.

He wondered what Melly would think of her brother's replacement. She probably wouldn't think of him as a replacement because she wasn't a part of their team. To her, Lolly had been a beloved little brother, her only remaining family. Now he was gone and she was alone. Kelsey felt an immediate stab of guilt because he hadn't called her once since the funeral, even after he had promised Lolly he would take care of her. But he couldn't do it, couldn't face her, couldn't look in Melly's face and see the possible blame and recrimination over his failure to protect her brother. It was to his advantage she hadn't been able to attend the rehearsal and subsequent dinner the previous evening due to some work event. Today would be the first time he had laid eyes on her in almost three months since Lolly's funeral, and he was nervous.

He was subdued as they arrived at the church, but the men were sequestered in a changing room because of course Nick's fiancée, Ashleigh, would do things the old-fashioned way and refuse to see her husband before the wedding. If ten years ago when they were newbies in basic together someone had told Kelsey Nick Lassiter would marry a virgin and wait to consummate their relationship until they were married, Kelsey would have laughed hysterically and told that person he was crazy. But Nick was doing exactly that, and he was ecstatically happy about it. And he was now Second Lieutenant Nick Lassiter, an actual officer. Things were changing and Kelsey wasn't sure he liked the new order. In fact, he was pretty sure he didn't. At least their team would soon be reunited. As soon as Nick returned from his honeymoon, they would officially be together again. Truck's injury and subsequent therapy had been the deciding factor in keeping them together. Since he was out of commission for the duration of Nick's officer training, Kelsey was given a desk job and told to wait for further instructions. But, being Kelsey, he hadn't been able to stand being behind a desk. Instead he had traded up and wormed his way back to sniper school, helping to train the newbies for the duration of his off time.

Nick finished Officer Candidate School and Travis Vega was assigned to their team. They had ten days to train without him and then Second Lieutenant Nick Lassiter would return and take charge of his team once again. Without Lolly, almost as if he had never existed.

The three men changed into their dress blues while Travis watched, looking bored. He had opted to come today for whatever reason, even though Kelsey had warned him there would be no booze because Ashleigh's father was a reverend who believed prohibition was the best cure for the country's many ills. Ashleigh and her little sister, Caleigh, had never even tasted alcohol, which was another reason to find it hilarious Nick was marrying into their family, Nick who had started drinking when he was eight and probably had the liver to prove it. But not anymore. Now Nick was as sober as the family he was marrying into though, to be fair, he had cut back on his drinking when they went to sniper school, not wanting anything to mess up his chances of becoming an H.O.G.

The last few years Kelsey could count on his hands the number of times Nick had more than a beer or two a week. So it wasn't as if he was curbing some entrenched lifestyle for his new wife who, in her defense, hadn't told him to quit drinking. In fact Ashleigh had told him to keep doing what he was doing, that he didn't have to change for her, but Nick had done it voluntarily because he had lost his interest in the stuff, which basically meant when Kelsey spent time at their house in the future—which he planned to do a lot because who else did he have—he would have to BYOB. So really, Nick's newfound dryness was more of an inconvenience to him, and that was probably why he was so irritated about it. Or maybe his issue went deeper. Maybe it was the fact that his best friend, the man who was like a brother to him, had found someone else, someone he loved more than Kelsey. On the surface of things, Kelsey liked Ashleigh. She was good for Nick. She had gotten him to go to Officer Candidate School. She had forced him to exorcize some old demons from his past. But she was also taking him away, and for that he hated her.

"You guys sure do look handsome," Vegas said. He sounded slightly inebriated, which made Kelsey wonder what was in the bottle of soda he had been sipping since they arrived. Nick and Ashton gave him a look, too, as if they weren't quite sure what to make of him. He had only arrived and moved in the previous week. It had been hard to let him move into Lolly's room, but it was a practical arrangement because with the loss of Nick and Lolly they needed the help with the rent. All of them were trying hard to refrain from judging, trying to refrain from comparing him to Lolly because if they did, they would hate him for sure. He was nothing like Lolly, but no one was. Lolly had been a little brother to them all, kind, unassuming, loyal, and capable in a dogfight. Not only was the new guy unproven in combat, but he seemed cocky and overbearing.

There was a knock on the door and Kelsey tensed, but it was only Caleigh with a box of boutonnieres.

"Hey, guys, how's it going in here?" she asked. She stepped into the room and set the box on a chair, rifling through until she located the largest arrangement. She pulled it out and held it aloft to Nick. "Want me to do this for you?"

"Yes," Nick said. "I haven't ever pinned one of these on."

"Not even for prom?" Caleigh asked.

"Oh, Caleigh, you don't want to hear about my prom experience. It will straighten your hair." He fluffed one of her curls, and she laughed. She was a pretty girl, *girl* being the operative word. Her innocence made her seem even younger than nineteen.

Travis hit Kelsey in the chest. "*Who is that?*" he mouthed.

Kelsey frowned at the look on his new teammate's face. "This is Caleigh Desmond," Kelsey said because she was standing in front of him now, fishing for his flower. "She's Ashleigh's little sister and Nick's soon-to-be sister-in-law." *Hint, hint, don't even think of it, moron.* She was also another reminder of Lolly because Lolly had been half in love with her, and the feeling had seemed to be mutual. He wondered then how Caleigh was doing, how she was coping with the loss and the knife of guilt twisted deeper in his chest.

"Hey, I'm Travis," the new guy said, apparently undeterred by Kelsey's not-so-subtle warning.

"Travis enjoys long walks in the rain and brushing puppies," Kelsey said. "Unfortunately this session of *The Dating Game* has reached its limit. I'll pin this on Truck because I did go to prom and I'm a pro. Run along now, sweetheart, and tend to your sister." He took the flower from Caleigh, put his arm around her shoulders and physically ushered her from the room, closing the door behind her. "Dude, no," he said to Vegas as soon as he turned around.

"What?" Vegas said, feigning innocence.

"Look, there are a million pretty women in the world, all of whom would probably line up to be with a marine. Leave that one alone," Kelsey said. He stopped short in front of Truck and pinned the flower on his lapel, doing it over when the orchid sagged and leaned to the right.

"I was looking," Travis said, sounding sullen. "A guy can look."

"Not at her," Kelsey said. "She's a baby."

"She looked pretty grown up to me," Travis said. Kelsey glanced at Nick and saw his fists were clenched and his mouth pressed together which meant he was letting Kelsey handle it so he didn't have to explode on his wedding day. Truck noticed and added his own two cents.

"You want to make it on this team, you'll leave Caleigh Desmond alone," he said, and it wasn't a request.

"Whatever," Travis said. It was already apparent he resented authority and restrictions. "I guess I could go for Lolly's sister. She's pretty smoking.'"

Truck put his hand on Kelsey's shoulder, which was the only thing that kept him from ripping the guy's head off. "I think you would do best to look outside the team for a woman," Truck said, purposely keeping his tone even.

"She's not really part of the team any more, you know, since..."

"She's part of the team," Kelsey yelled, shrugging away from Truck's clasp. "She'll always be part of the team, and I swear if you so much as breathe on her I will find twelve different ways to kill you slowly while you sleep. Either sit there and shut up or get out and go troll for a woman who is available."

"Oh, I see how it is," Travis said, holding up his hands in surrender with a smug grin that belied his forced humility. "Fine, I'll go stake out a seat." He left and the three remaining marines released a pent-up sigh of relief.

"He's a kid," Nick said.

"He's twenty three," Kelsey replied. "Lolly's age."

"But he's not Lolly," Ashton said. "This kid is untested and trying desperately to make us like him."

"That was him trying to make us like him?" Kelsey asked. "If so, someone needs to give him a lesson."

"He's all attitude and mouth," Nick replied. "We'll rub off the rough edges. Maybe there's something worthwhile underneath." They remained staring at the door, missing Lolly. They knew it wasn't fair to compare the new kid to the guy he was replacing, but they did it anyway and found him lacking in every way.

There was another knock on the door. Kelsey took a breath and forced himself to answer, steeling himself for the sight of Melly, but it wasn't Melly; it was Shelby. He was glad he had steeled himself, though, because the sight of her was almost as painful and shocking. The last time any of them saw her was a few months ago in the hospital in Germany after they rescued her from captors who brutally and repeatedly raped her. Then she had been shell-shocked and injured. Now she looked like a different person, fresh-faced, pretty, and smiling. But she was yet another reminder of Lolly because he had died protecting her, died while trying to get her to safety aboard a chopper.

Kelsey didn't realize he was staring at her until Truck pushed him out of the way and picked her up, holding her close while he buried his face in her hair. She returned the hug, closing her eyes as a couple of tears leaked out and rolled down her cheeks.

"Hey," Truck said. His voice sounded as broken and ragged as Kelsey felt.

"Hey," Shelby whispered.

"Missed you," Truck said.

"You have no idea," Shelby replied. Truck chuckled and set her down long enough to close the door behind them, blocking their reunion from Nick and Kelsey's prying eyes.

Kelsey turned to Nick with a frown. "Are they really together?" Kelsey asked.

"Yeah," Nick said, and he was smiling in that new sappy way he had, as if he was in on a secret and had appreciated glimpsing the love fest that had just taken place.

"I don't get it," Kelsey said.

"What's not to get?" Nick said. He turned to inspect himself in the full-length mirror, tugging on his cufflinks.

"We rescued her," Kelsey said. "Truck knows what they did to her."

"Yeah, so?"

Nick really didn't get it, but how to explain? "How could he want to be with her, knowing what they did to her?" Kelsey asked.

Nick frowned at him in the mirror. "What are you talking about?"

"Dude, you know what I'm talking about. We know exactly what those monsters did to her, and yet Truck is out there kissing her like she's as untouched as Caleigh."

Nick turned. "Are you saying it was Shelby's fault she was raped?" He whispered, not wanting Truck and Shelby to hear their discussion.

"Of course not," Kelsey said.

"Then, what, she's tainted because of it?" Nick clarified.

"No, not at all," Kelsey said. "It wasn't her fault, and I wish her the best. But it's a lot of baggage for Truck to handle, don't you think?"

Nick shrugged. "If anyone can handle it, then Truck can."

"But why should he have to? Why shouldn't he find a nice girl who doesn't have issues?"

"Everyone has issues, Kelse," Nick said. "And Shelby is who Truck loves. She's his choice. Have you ever seen him act like this with anyone else?"

"No, but it seems like a lot for a guy to take on. I don't get why he doesn't find someone else. Why does it have to be up to us men to cure the women of the world? Why can't they come to us unbroken?"

"You can't always choose who to fall in love with," Nick said. "Sometimes love takes you by surprise, and sometimes that surprise is the best thing that ever happened to you." He looked at the mirror again, giving himself a goofy grin as he no doubt thought about Ashleigh.

"I threw up in my mouth a little," Kelsey said.

"That's because you have a hangover," Nick said.

"Wow, Reverend Desmond, when did you start to look exactly like your new son-in-law?"

"I wasn't preaching," Nick said, noting Kelsey's testy tone. "I was making an observation. Get wasted if you want, but don't come crying to me when you feel like you were hit by a bus the next day."

Kelsey sat, giving the chair across from him a sullen kick. "Is this what it's going to be like from now on? You and Truck self-righteous and *in love*?"

"You'll always have the new guy," Nick said, grinning as he sat across from his best friend. "Or, I don't know, you could join our ranks, find a woman, and get married."

"Dude, seriously, I will run out that door and leave you at the altar if you ever say those words to me again. I have years and years and years of dating ahead of me before I reach this point." He flicked his hand at Nick, a derisive sneer on his face.

"You know what's funny? You feel sorry for me. You think I've somehow been blinded by Ashleigh, but the truth is my eyes are open for the first time. This is what life is about, this dedicating yourself to someone else, building a family, making the world a better place. For the first time in my life I'm exactly where I'm supposed to be, where I want to be, doing what I want to do, and it feels great. I don't feel like I'm giving anything up; I feel like I'm gaining everything."

Kelsey held up his hands, palms out. "I'm not drinking the kool-aid, so you can stop trying to offer me a cup. You and Truck want to tie the noose around your necks and take the plunge, have at it. But I have no intention of settling down anytime this century."

Nick shrugged. "Suit yourself. You have no idea how much you're missing."

Kelsey shook his head. "I don't know what kind of brain fever has consumed you, but I don't want it. Weird. It's like you've been taken over by aliens and you're freaking me out, so stop."

"Fine," Nick said. He sat back and they stared at each other until Kelsey grinned.

"You're thinking about the honeymoon, *amIright?*"

Nick blew out a puff of air that might have passed for an uncomfortable chuckle. "Yeah, I'm thinking about it. I'm nervous, if you want the truth."

"Nervous? Why? You're not the virgin. You've had like a bajillion years experience."

"I know, but it's Ashleigh's first time, and I want things to go well for her. You know what a woman's first time can be like. I don't want to hurt her."

"Whatever." Kelsey didn't understand most of what Nick said lately. Somehow he had gone from hard-partying Marine recruit to a buttoned down officer who was marrying a virgin. And not only was he marrying what had to be the last twenty-something virgin on the planet, but he was *worried* about it. Kelsey had a sinking feeling like maybe his friendship with Nick was coming to an end. Ashton hadn't mentioned marriage to Shelby, but they all knew he was thinking it because he had that same sappy, over-the-moon look Nick had been wearing since he met Ashleigh. With Lolly gone, where did that leave Kelsey? Getting drunk with the newbie on a daily basis? No, thank you.

Ashton returned and looked in the mirror as he adjusted his bowtie. "We ran into Caleigh. She said they're ready for us. I'm going to go meet up with Melly, and I'll see you guys at the altar." He surprised Kelsey by pulling Nick into a hug and giving his back a couple of pats. It was a manly sort of hug, but Truck wasn't known for being affectionate. This was probably a symptom of the changes Shelby had made in him. They had been talking daily during the last few months of their separation, and they had been seeking counseling, too. There had been times over the last few weeks when the usually taciturn and closed-off Ashton would start a sentence with "My therapist says I should…" "Love you, man," he said now to Nick while Kelsey stared in amazement.

"Back at you," Nick replied, his voice going a little husky as he cleared his throat and looked out the window, squinting at the sun to try and cover the sudden moisture in his eyes. And now Kelsey was looking anywhere but at them because all he could think was how Lolly would have loved this moment, Lolly, who never had any trouble telling them he loved them, who had never felt the need to cover his feelings with an open display of masculinity. Finally Truck left and Nick cleared his throat again, but before they could go out, the door was opened and Reverend and Mrs. Desmond stepped inside.

Reverend Desmond was one of those men who instilled fear in those around them, especially if they were up to no good as Kelsey usually was. He found himself standing taller and resisting the urge to salute as the older man came into the room. But this was the day for surprises because he made his way to his future son-in-law and gave him a bear hug.

"Nick, I'm getting ready to walk my daughter down the aisle, but I wanted to slip in and tell you how happy we are you're our son after this day. We love you."

"We do," Mrs. Desmond said, chorusing her agreement. And now Nick wasn't even pretending not to cry. Instead he threw himself at his soon-to-be father-in-law and wept on his shoulder while Mrs. Desmond joined their party and made a group hug. Which left Kelsey once again standing on the outside looking in and feeling awkward, at least until Mrs. Desmond noticed him and opened her arm, indicating him forward. Tentatively he stepped closer and was absorbed into their hug. Once again his thoughts flashed to Melly because it was the same sort of hug she had given him when he arrived back in the states after Lolly's death. She had pulled his head to her chest and held him, offering complete comfort and absolution, and, for the thirty seconds he had allowed himself to accept it, he had been free. Then all the old guilt and self-recrimination had come flooding back, and he had pushed her away, like he was about to do now because he couldn't go down this road of being free with his emotions—not now, maybe not ever.

"If we're going to sing *Kumbaya*, then someone is going to have to teach me the words because I don't know them," he said. Nick and Mr. and Mrs. Desmond laughed, breaking up the hug as the two older adults left the room. "Ready?" Kelsey said, giving Nick a chance to compose himself. Not that it mattered much because he was fairly certain the guy would lose it again as soon as he caught sight of his bride.

"Ready," Nick said, scrubbing his eyes with the heels of his hands. The pastor who would be performing the ceremony met them at the door and led them into the crowded sanctuary. Most of the crowd consisted of family and friends of Ashleigh and her parents. Nick's side of the aisle contained a handful of marines and his mother, a spacy hippy he hadn't seen in six years. He looked surprised to see her there today because she hadn't shown up at the rehearsal dinner the night before, nor had she replied to the invitation. As far as Kelsey knew, she wasn't planning to attend or maybe hadn't received the invitation. And now here she was. Surprise!

Nick pulled his attention away from his mother, who was waving at him like he was the star in a parade, and focused on the processional. Kelsey's attention was rooted to the door, too, because he knew it was going to be Truck and Melly. The double doors opened, and there she was, wearing the ubiquitous pink bridesmaid's dress that somehow managed to look good on her. Maybe it was her dark skin or well-rounded figure. Or maybe it was the truckloads of dark hair she had fastened into some intricate updo that probably took an hour to arrange and yet looked casual, as if she had haphazardly tossed it into a clip and added some pins. Whatever the case, she looked breathtakingly, heart-stoppingly beautiful, so much so that Kelsey's air left him in a rush and he stared unblinkingly as she made her way down the aisle.

She didn't look at him, though. She focused on Nick, smiling in a demure way that let Kelsey know her mind was on the upcoming nuptials as his probably should be. Truck deposited her at her assigned spot before turning to land behind Kelsey. The doors opened again, and this time Caleigh made her way down the aisle. She was a beautiful girl, but she held no interest for Kelsey. She was too young, too innocent, and too much Nick's sister-in-law. Instead he saw her in a brotherly way and gave her an appropriately patronizing smile and wink when he caught her eye. She smiled and stood across from him, turning expectantly toward the doors like everyone else.

The flower girl emerged—a cute three-year-old cousin of Ashleigh's who took her job seriously, portioning out exactly four flowers every couple of feet until she reached the front of the church. She found her piece of tape on the floor and stood on it as if afraid to move.

And then it was Ashleigh's turn. The room was already quiet, but it became even more hushed when the doors opened to reveal Ashleigh on the arm of Reverend Desmond. Her face was covered by a blusher but that didn't seem to matter to Nick who was once again unabashedly crying.

"Geez," Kelsey muttered, fishing in his pocket for a tissue. He handed it over with a whispered, "Man up, Marine," that made Nick laugh as he wiped his eyes. Ashleigh reached the front of the church and Nick and Kelsey turned toward her, which also meant Kelsey was now facing Melly. She glanced at him, smiling, tears sparkling on her long, thick lashes. Kelsey winked, and her smile widened before her focus turned to Nick and Ashleigh. His heart felt lighter. Maybe things with Melly would be okay.

The ceremony was short, and then it was time for the kiss. The thirty or so marines in attendance sent up an enthusiastic "Oorah!" Ashleigh's side of the church jumped in alarm and stared, and then it was time for the recessional. Truck and Melly met up and walked out. Kelsey retrieved Caleigh and followed behind.

"So tell me about the new guy," Caleigh said with forced casualness.

"His name is Mr. Off-Limits-To-You, but we call him So-Much-As-Look-At-Caleigh-And-We'll-Kill-You."

Caleigh rolled her eyes. "Is this the part of the wedding where you tell me I didn't gain one brother-in-law, I gained two?"

"Look around, Sweetheart," Kelsey said, pointing to the rows of marines on Nick's side of the aisle. "You gained a whole battalion."

"I'm a grownup, Kelsey," Caleigh said.

"If you have to say the words, then you can't possibly mean them," Kelsey pointed out. "But it's okay, Caleigh. We like you little and innocent, at least for a while longer. Don't be in any hurry to grow up. The world is a big, scary place."

"I'm nineteen and getting really tired of everyone treating me like a baby," Caleigh said.

"Honey, when I was your age, I felt the same way. But now, almost a decade later, I wish there had been someone standing protectively over my shoulder, trying to make sure I went the right way."

"I think you turned out all right," Caleigh said, smiling up at him with her trademark sweetness and innocence.

"That's because you only see what's on the outside. On the inside, I'm a dark, twisted, and tortured soul."

Caleigh laughed, which was ironic considering Kelsey was being serious for once. He deposited her with her parents and went to form the honor guard for the sword ceremony. Since it was a dry reception, it was being held in the fellowship hall of the church. Kelsey, Truck, Travis, and a handful of other marines stood at the entrance, right hands on their sabers. As best man and second in command, it was Kelsey's job to call it.

"Marines, swords out," he called. Eight sabers were unsheathed, criss-crossing in an arch over the entryway, tips touching as Ashleigh and Nick made their way down the line. Kelsey and Truck were at the end. They crossed their swords, stopping Nick and Ashleigh's progress and then lifted them again after they kissed. After they passed through, Kelsey took his sword and swatted Ashleigh on the behind.

"Welcome to the marines, Ma'am," he said, smiling. "Return," he called, and the marines sheathed their swords, waiting until they were all in line so the last few inches were made together with a single click as the sabers locked back into place.

CHAPTER 2

Melly was avoiding him. Or maybe Kelsey was avoiding her. All he knew was that they were sitting at the head table a few spaces apart and so far hadn't said a word to each other. Then again there had been a lot going on, and there was more to come. After grabbing a quick bite and saying a few words, they would have to take some pictures.

Caleigh stood to give the toast, some girly drivel that made Ashleigh and Melly sniffle, and then it was his turn. He had always assumed he would be drunk when this moment came, but here he was: stone cold sober and trying to pretend he had some idea what to say.

"A decade ago I joined the marines. My first day in basic, I was prepared to be the screwup because that had been my M/O all through school. Then I met this guy at the same time the drill sergeant did. We both took in his smirk and arm full of tats and I knew I had found my salvation. The sergeant zeroed in on Nick, hating him with a passion for whatever reason, and I was free to slip under the radar. So I figured if I hitched my wagon to his, I might get a free pass through life because who was going to pay attention to me with a guy like that standing by my side? Only it didn't work out according to my plan because beneath all the tats and the fierce expression the guy turned out to be ambitious and ethical, urging me through basic and every training since then, leading me through life on and off the field. So to you, my brother, I say congratulations, and thank you for the lessons." He tipped his glass of water, wishing for champagne instead as he took a sip and set it down.

"Pictures," Caleigh whispered. Someone had apparently appointed her the wedding coordinator because everyone stood to follow her back to the sanctuary.

"That was sweet, Jaws," Melly said, slinking up beside him.

"I'm a sweet person, Melly." He resisted the urge to reach out and rest his hand on her shoulders.

"When you want to be," she said. "Which isn't often enough in my experience." Her teasing tone made him more comfortable, as if they were getting back on solid footing. And then she continued. "So, how are you?"

Not good. "Fine. How are you?"

"Fine." Was she lying, too? He had almost worked up the nerve to ask her when she stopped at a table and spoke. Since they were in the middle of a conversation, Kelsey stopped with her, not realizing the person she was speaking to was a man until he was accidentally eavesdropping. "Hey, Robert, we're going to take some pictures. The rumor is it won't take too long. Would you like to come and watch, or are you content to stay here until I return?"

"I'll stay," Robert said. "I didn't get lunch today, and I'm starving."

Melly smiled. "Picking food over me already. Not good." She squeezed his shoulder and something in Kelsey's midsection twisted and froze.

"What the crud, Melly? You brought a date?" he hissed as they walked away.

She looked up at him in confusion. "Uh, yeah. Why do you make it sound like that's weird?"

"Because it is," he said.

"Why? Didn't you bring a date? I thought you would have a string of bimbettes lined up, jostling for the opportunity."

"No, I…" *I thought you were my date.* Hearing the words in his head made him realize how ridiculous they were. They hadn't spoken a word in almost four months. Why would he think she had been on the same page? Why would he think she would be as keen to see him as he had been to see her? He knew it wasn't rational, but he was still blisteringly angry. "Well that's great, Melly."

"What is your problem?" she asked.

"Do you really think you should be dating so soon? Shouldn't there be some sort of requisite mourning period?" He knew as soon as the words were out of his mouth they were both ridiculous and a mistake, but of course he didn't take them back because this was Melly, and Kelsey had long ago formed a do-or-die philosophy with her.

"Un-be-lievable, Kelsey. You haven't changed at all. I don't know why I was stupid enough to believe maybe you had."

"Newsflash, Luscious, I don't need to change. I'm perfect the way I am."

"The sad part is that you believe that," Melly said. "And aren't I the idiot for believing and praying Lolly's death would be a wakeup call."

"Uh, guys, everything okay?" Ashleigh asked. They had reached the sanctuary and were now having their brawl in front of their assembled group of friends. Melly turned her back on him and stormed away.

"We're not through," Kelsey called.

She said something in Spanish and went to stand in her assigned spot beside Caleigh while Kelsey took his spot beside Nick.

"The blond marine looks like he's growling," the photographer said, and Kelsey pasted on a smile. Either the tension was so thick the photographer hurried or he really had planned to go that quickly because the pictures were finished in a short period of time.

The group followed Nick and Ashleigh back to the fellowship hall for the cake cutting ceremony and ubiquitous first dances. Kelsey tried to corner Melly in order to pick up their conversation, but she was with the man. Instead he set up camp in the corner and unabashedly stared. Who was the man? How long had they been dating? Did she love him?

The dancing began, but Robert and Melly made no move to take the floor. By the hopeful glances she was sending in Robert's direction, Kelsey knew Melly was longing to be on the dance floor, and for once he decided to give her what she wanted.

"Dance, Melly?" He made it more of a command than a request, and she stared up at him, her lips pressed together in a grim line as she tried to decide whether or not she was going to comply.

"Fine," she said at last, thrusting her hand into his as he led her to the dance floor. It was a slow song, which worked well since he planned to talk, but once she was in his arms, he forgot what he wanted to say.

"You really look beautiful," he said instead.

She blinked up at him in confusion a few times. "Uh, thank you?"

He smiled. "What? I'm not allowed to be angry and compliment you at the same time? You should know by now I'm a multi-tasker."

"I know you can be charming when you want to be," Melly said.

"Why is it when you say stuff like that it doesn't sound like a compliment?" he asked.

"Because it's not. Because I can tell when you're being real and when you're not. Most of the time you're a big fake, and it makes me crazy."

"So what do you want me to do? Walk around with my heart on my sleeve all the time like some kind of loser?" he asked.

"Yes."

"Not gonna happen, Melly."

"I know, Kelsey," she said. "But a girl can dream, can't she?"

"I don't get you," he said. "You're not like other women."

"I'm not like *your* other women, which is a very good thing. And I know you don't understand me. That's our problem—you don't understand me, and I understand you too well."

"We don't have a problem," he said. "We're fine."

"Yes, Kelsey, everything is fine. We're fine, I'm fine, you're fine. You're not grieving and suffering Post Traumatic Stress Disorder."

His grip tightened on her waist. "I'm not. Don't joke."

"I'm not joking because you are, and you know it. How are you sleeping? Well?"

"Some nights," he said.

"The nights you knock yourself out with a dozen beers, you mean? Those nights?"

"You're pretty well versed on my life for someone who hasn't been in it for the past quarter of a year," he said.

"I couldn't," she said.

"Why not?" They weren't even pretending to dance anymore. Instead they were well on their way to becoming a distraction. Melly turned and left the room, Kelsey close on her heels in case she was of a mind to escape. She ducked out of sight into the coat room and rounded on him.

"You know why," she hissed.

He stared at her, blinking, his worst fears coming true. "Because you blame me," he muttered.

Her jaw dropped. "What? Kelsey, no, that's not it. How could you think that?"

"Because it's true," he said. He turned away from her and she grabbed his bicep, anchoring him in place.

"No. It's not. Look at me."

He shook his head.

"Look at me," she commanded.

He turned to look at her, and the pain must have been written on his face because she winced. "Kelsey, don't. Don't do this to yourself. Please."

He shook his head again and tried to retreat, but she wouldn't let him.

"No," she said, and then she stood on her toes and kissed him.

It had been three years since she kissed him that first time, but he remembered everything about her like it was yesterday, the feel of her in his arms, the taste of her, the softness of her lips. And the feeling, the unmistakable feeling of being with Melly, as if everything was temporarily okay in his world, as if the pain was on hold. He should have kept his mouth shut and kept kissing her but, being Kelsey, he couldn't. "Melly," he breathed, cinching her closer. "I need you. I need this."

Melly froze. "This?"

"This. You and me. Together. This." He tried to kiss her again, but she leaned away from him, looking up at him with luminous eyes. The kiss had knocked loose a strand of her hair and she brushed at it.

"What is this to you?" she asked.

Now it was his turn to back away. "Whoa, one kiss in three years and you're pushing for a definition? That's not how I operate."

She pinned him with a stare, and he resisted the urge to squirm under her scrutiny. "No, it's not. Too bad for me I know exactly how you operate. I can't believe this. I can't believe I was so stupid to get sucked in to your charm when I supposedly know better."

"What are you talking about?" Kelsey asked.

"You know exactly what I'm talking about," Melly said. "I'm talking about the fact that I am not one of your flavors of the week. I deserve better than this, better than you."

Ouch. "Why are you suddenly too good for me?" he asked. "It's not like you have a string of men beating down your door."

"And do you know why that is? Because I'm not willing to settle for guys like you, men who want a quick hookup in the coatroom of a wedding and nothing more. Maybe I'm picky, but my heart is intact, and I plan to keep it that way." She shoved at his chest and he took a step back.

"Your heart isn't intact, baby, it's ice cold."

"No, it's off limits to you, and you can't stand it because I'm possibly the one woman in the world smart enough to resist you."

"Resist me? You haven't resisted me because I haven't tried. Here's something for you to think about, Mellisandra: both times we've kissed you've been the aggressor. That doesn't sound like someone who is trying too hard to get away. You're the one with a problem here."

They faced off a foot apart, her hands on her hips, her chest heaving. At last some of her anger faded away, leaving sadness. "It didn't have to be like this, Kelsey. It didn't have to end this way."

"What ending?" he asked. For him, this was a normal day, another fight.

But Melly didn't answer; she simply shook her head and walked away. Kelsey leaned against the wall and sank to the floor, feeling oddly empty. What had that been about, and why had it felt so final? He was about to put on a happy face and go back to the party when another couple entered the coatroom and began loudly making out.

Kelsey's lip wrinkled in disgust. Was that what he and Melly had looked and sounded like? If so, gross. He was slightly embarrassed over having placed her in the position of being the woman who was groped in the coatroom, but his embarrassment quickly gave way to outrage because the woman giggled and he recognized the sound.

He strode forward and peeled the couple apart, holding Travis in one hand and Caleigh in the other. "What are you doing?" he addressed Vegas.

"What does it look like?" Vegas asked with no remorse, and no wonder—he was drunk. Worse, Caleigh was, too.

"You got her *drunk?*" Kelsey asked, outraged as Caleigh giggled again.

"She had a few sips," Travis said. "Not enough to get her drunk."

"She's never had alcohol before," Kelsey said. "Of course it was enough to get her drunk. What are you thinking? This is your team leader's little sister. You've got to think, man." He turned to Caleigh. "Go find Melly." Melly would know what to do; she would take care of her. He watched her walk away and rounded on Travis. "I should beat you senseless for that."

Travis withdrew a flask from his jacket. "You could. Or..." He held out the flask to Kelsey. Kelsey stared at it, debating. He had spent the day doing his duty as best man, being reasonable and congratulatory when he really wanted to drown his sorrows and hide. The thing with Melly had been too much, and now he was ready for some numbness.

"You're lucky I have a weakness for unknown substances in dirty flasks," Kelsey said. He took the flask and tipped it back, noting as he did that it was the hard, cheap stuff that should work in no time flat.

Good, he thought. The sooner he forgot this day, the better he would feel.

* * *

THE NEXT MORNING A DOOR SLAMMED, and Kelsey realized it was his own. He groaned, but whoever it was paid him no attention because soon the shades were drawn and a cruel stream of light flooded his room. It could only be Truck, but he had no idea why Truck would be stomping around his room, trying to kill him with sunlight.

"Ashton," he muttered, covering his head with his pillow.

"No, not Ashton," Melly growled. She grabbed the pillow and beat him in the head with it a few times before tossing it away.

Kelsey reluctantly opened his eyes and stared at her, clutching the sheet over his midsection as he suddenly wished he were the type who wore clothes to bed. "Melly, what are you doing here?"

"I really don't know," she said. She put her hands on her hips and stared down at him. She was wearing a form-fitting t-shirt and jeans that hugged her curves, a departure from her usual buttoned-down after-work appearance. "No, wait, scratch that. I came to tell you goodbye."

"Goodbye? Where are you going?" he mumbled. He looked around for something, anything to alleviate the burning in his throat. What exactly had he drunk last night? It was all a hazy fog.

Melly barked a harsh laugh. "You don't remember anything, do you?"

He squinted at her, trying hard to remember. "You kissed me."

"I guess you would remember that part. But you don't remember what came after."

He shook his head as his apprehension grew. What had he done? How had he gotten home?

"You and the new kid got drunk in the coatroom of the church. While everyone else was dancing and celebrating Nick and Ashleigh, you were hiding out and getting drunk like an eighteen-year-old frat boy."

"What's the big deal? I had a few drinks."

"A few drinks wouldn't have been a big deal. You got wasted, stupid drunk, and stumbled out, making a fool of yourself, a fool of me, and causing a scene. You don't remember talking to me, to Robert?"

"Who is Robert?" he asked, scraping his tongue over the roof of his mouth, trying to conjure some moisture.

"He was my date and a nice guy and you humiliated him by announcing to the world at large what happened with us in the coatroom. You humiliated me. You *hurt* me."

He stared up at her in amazement because there was hurt in her eyes, along with tears. Melly was usually careful, composed, and cool. Not today. The pain in her eyes was raw, and he had put it there. "I'm sorry," he murmured.

"Not nearly as sorry as I am, Kelsey. My brother…." Her voice broke. She took a shaky breath and started again. "My brother loved you. He only saw the good in you, the potential. It was something we argued about on a frequent basis. So while I would love nothing better than to write you off and never see your stupidly handsome face again, I owe it to Jesus to say this one last thing: He didn't die so you could live your life this way."

"What way, Melly? It's no big deal. So I got a little drunk at a wedding. It happens"

"A little drunk?" she repeated, outraged. "You passed out, Kelsey. Nick was so worried he wanted to bring you home himself and miss the first night of his honeymoon. Instead his father-in-law did it. That's right—Truck and Reverend Desmond carried you home and tucked you into bed. Naked because, did I mention, you did a little strip routine at the church?"

Kelsey was blushing, and he never blushed. It took a lot to embarrass him, and now he was beyond embarrassed; he was mortified.

"So I came here today to ask you to get help because you need it," Melly said.

He stared at her, noting her cool detachment with anger. "And that's it. You need help, Kelsey. Goodbye."

"That pretty much sums it up," she said.

"Wow, you're a great friend, Melly. Lolly would be proud," he said, heavy on the sarcasm.

Her fists clenched, and he wondered if she was going to deck him. He almost hoped she would because maybe it would ease the horrible gnawing sensation in his chest. She was disappointed in him, and she was going away. He wasn't sure which hurt more.

"You think I'm cold," she said.

"Baby, I know it," he snapped.

"You know nothing. You see nothing beyond your own pretty face. Don't you think I'm tempted by you? Don't you think I feel the attraction between us? Do you think I'm oblivious?"

He had no answer to any of those questions, so he simply stared at her in amazement while she continued.

"There's a not so small part of me that, even now, even when I'm so angry at you I want to beat you, wants to crawl in beside you and kiss you. To hold you and caress you and try and soothe whatever is eating you alive. But I can't. I can't fix you, and I won't lose myself trying. You are broken; I get it. But maybe, just maybe, I am, too. Maybe I want someone to hold me and pick up my shattered pieces and tell me it's going to be okay. Maybe I was desperately hoping it would be you. Maybe when I lost my brother, the one person on earth who meant anything to me, the one family member I had left, maybe I wanted you to be there. Maybe I wanted to lay my head on your chest and weep with someone who knew and loved him as much as I did. But you weren't there. You were licking your manufactured guilt and dealing with your grief in your own selfish way. For four months I waited for your call, Kelsey, dying a little more when it didn't come. How could you do that to me? How could you leave me that alone?"

He opened his mouth, and she shook her head.

"Don't, just don't. I don't want to hear your answers or your excuses because I already know. You're broken. I hope you get help. I hope you get fixed. But I'm not going to be the one to do it." She turned and headed for the door.

Kelsey sat up. "Melly, don't. Don't go. I…I could hold you now." He reached out his arms, holding them wide.

She paused and looked at him, considering. He could see the temptation playing across her features as she debated with herself. It was the first time he had ever glimpsed her vulnerability, and it sliced him open inside. For the last few months he had avoided her, telling himself she was okay because Melly was always okay. But she wasn't okay; he could see that now. She had been hurting, emotionally bloody and raw, and he had ignored her. What did that say about him?

At last she came to a resolution. "No. It's too late for that, too late for us. Get better, okay? For Jesus because he loved you and he believed in you." Her voice broke again and she took another shaky breath. Her hand gripped the doorframe so tightly her knuckles turned white. "My brother believed in you so much. You have no idea. Don't make a liar out of him." With that, she turned and let herself out of his room, tears streaming silently down her cheeks.

CHAPTER 3

For two weeks, Kelsey remained defiant. Nick was on his honeymoon and Ashton was busy with Shelby. Things were going so well she decided to move to North Carolina and room with Melly. That left Travis, the new guy. All he wanted to do was get drunk, and Kelsey was happy to comply. The two weeks were a blur of alcohol and puking, and then Nick arrived home.

"Get help, or you're off the team," were his best friend's greeting words as soon as he showed up at work his first morning back.

"What?" Kelsey asked, sure he had misunderstood.

"You heard me, Jaws."

"You're not serious," Kelsey said.

"I'm dead serious."

"How come you're not saying this to the new guy?" he asked. Travis was as hung over as he was; he had to be because they had consumed the same amount of liquor the night before.

"Because the new guy is still functioning. Because the new guy isn't my spotter. Because the new guy isn't my best friend. Because the new guy doesn't have PTSD."

"One *because* would have sufficed," Kelsey said, pressing his palm to his head in a vain attempt to make the pain go away.

"You want to joke, Kelse, that's fine; you can do it from your shrink's office. I'm placing you on leave starting immediately."

Kelsey's jaw dropped and his fist clenched. "Is that how it's going to be now, *Lieutenant?*"

"Yes. Now get out of here so I can deal with the paperwork," Nick said. He turned away with a disgusted sigh and Kelsey began to realize maybe he was serious.

"How could you do this to me?" he asked.

"Because I love you, and because if I don't do this you're going to lose your career and maybe your life. Because more lives than yours are counting on you."

"Because is your new favorite word," Kelsey said. He swallowed down a lump of fear and tried to think. "What do I have to do to stay on the team?"

"Talk to a shrink. Start sleeping. Stop drinking. Shave, shower, and rejoin the world of the living."

Kelsey looked down at himself with a grimace. Was it really that apparent that he hadn't slept or showered in a few days? He thought he covered with a splash of cologne and a gallon of coffee. "I've been trying to sleep; I can't. The only thing that helps is the booze."

"I wasn't kidding about the Post Traumatic Stress, Jaws. I think your brain is frozen on that moment Lolly died, and I think you need help to get over it. Therapy did a lot of good for Truck. If I didn't think it could help you, I wouldn't suggest it."

Kelsey sank into a chair. "Melly left."

"What do you mean she left? Ashleigh talked to her yesterday. She said she's enjoying having Shelby as a roommate."

"I mean she left. *Me.* She left me."

Nick sat and faced his oldest friend. "Do you remember any of my wedding?"

"Everything until the end," Kelsey said. "I remember Melly kissed me. Then she left me in the coatroom."

"Then you came out of the coatroom. You said some things, some awful things. To Melly."

"What did I say?" His heart thumped with preemptive dread.

"You basically announced to the room at large you had made out with her in the coatroom. Then you told her the reason you weren't together was because she's fat."

"What?" Kelsey said. "She's not fat."

"You also used a racial slur."

Kelsey didn't have to ask which one. There was only one that might apply to a Hispanic female. "No. I've never said that word in my life. I would never," Kelsey said.

"Maybe you would never when you're sober. I guess I never realized how much of a mean drunk you are because we were usually drunk together. But let me be the first to tell you you're a mean drunk. I don't like you when you're wasted."

Kelsey thought he might throw up, and it had nothing to do with his hangover. Had he really said those awful things to Melly? How could he when he didn't believe them? How was it possible to undergo such a drastic alteration of personality?

"No wonder she wants nothing more to do with me."

"She doesn't want you out of her life, Kelse. She wants you to get help."

"That's not what she said," Kelsey replied.

"You said things you didn't mean, too. Call her. Apologize. Make up and move on," Nick suggested.

"Maybe it's better this way. Melly and I…we're toxic."

"You don't have to be," Nick said. "And you shouldn't give up three years of close friendship because of one argument."

"It's not the argument," Kelsey said. "It's everything." The guilt. The fear. Everything.

"Take some time. Think it over," Nick urged. "Melly is family. Who else do we have besides her, and who else does she have besides us? We orphans have to stick together."

"You're not part of the orphan club. Don't try to horn in, Lassiter."

"Close enough," Nick said. "My mother now believes she was abducted by aliens in Nevada. Did you know she cornered Ashleigh at the wedding and tried to get money to have the probe taken out of her head?"

"Whoa, time to up the meds," Kelsey said.

"Or stop taking them. She dropped so much acid when I was a kid. I think her circuits are permanently fried." Nick sighed and rubbed his hand over his eyes. "You know what the worst part is? It's going to be up to me to take care of her. She didn't take care of me when I was a kid, couldn't have cared less whether I lived or died, and now that she's getting older and sick I'm going to have to step up and do the right thing."

"You don't have to," Kelsey said. "No one would blame you if you didn't."

"Have you met my wife?" Nick asked. "She's already been talking about it as if it's a foregone conclusion. She wants us to look for a house with a mother-in-law suite in case my mom has to move in with us."

"Dude, your woman isn't normal. I tried to tell you not to marry her," Kelsey said.

"Yeah, well, it might interest you to know she's also preparing a Kelsey suite for when you wind up old and alone," Nick said. "And she's been cooking extra food and stocking our freezer to feed you guys."

"Like I said, the woman is a saint. Good thing you married her." He stood. "I guess I'll go call Truck's shrink." He paused, waiting to see if Nick would renege the command.

"Good. Let me know how it goes," Nick said, and Kelsey let himself out of the office. He stood in the hallway for a minute, dazed. How could he be a hairsbreadth from losing his career? He had always been the resilient jokester. When had that changed? Some guys in boot camp had been so intense they were a shoe-in for a strait jacket eventually. Not Kelsey. The drill sergeants, training, even killing men had rolled off his back like drops of water. Intellectually he had been prepared for the death of a friend or teammate. Why, then, was it hitting so hard?

With nothing left to do, he looked up the name of Truck's shrink and gave her a call. He was hoping she would say she was booked solid and unable to see him for a couple of months, but no such luck.

"I have an opening this afternoon. Why don't you come on over?"

"Great," Kelsey said, his dismal tone letting her know it wasn't great at all. He hung up and stared at his phone, trying to work up the nerve to call Melly. He should apologize for so many things, for calling her an unforgivable name, for publicly humiliating her, for abandoning her after Lolly made him swear to take care of her. Maybe he should simply apologize for existing and cover all his bases at once. In the end, he did nothing. He tucked his phone in his pocket and went to therapy, hating himself for being a coward.

He was nervous as he sat in the therapist's waiting room, and Kelsey was almost never nervous. His leg bounced, bobbing up and down as if detached from his body. The therapist called his name and he jumped, curling his hands into fists to try and gain some control.

"Kelsey, I'm Marilyn. Pleased to meet you." She held out her hand to shake. "I've heard a lot about you from Ashton."

"It's all lies," Kelsey said. "I'm not responsible for his crazy. Besides, I thought it was confidential."

"Therapy is confidential, but a conversation about how much he loves his best friends is not," Marilyn replied, smiling. "I promise, he didn't say anything bad." She motioned to the leather couch and Kelsey hesitated, not sure what he was supposed to do.

"Am I supposed to lie down?"

"If you like. Or you can sit. Whatever is most comfortable for you," Marilyn said. She sat in the chair beside the couch, and he sat, too, perching on the edge as if he might flee anytime the questions became too uncomfortable.

"This morning on the phone you mentioned your team leader is concerned about your wellbeing. Would this be Nick, the one you call Whit?"

Either Marilyn had done her homework, or she remembered everything Truck might have told her. Kelsey nodded. "Yes. He's my best friend, besides Truck."

"And Lolly," she added. "Ashton told me about him."

"I don't want to talk about him," Kelsey said, his fingers curling on the edge of the sofa as he dug in.

"All right, for now. I don't believe in starting off with a bang, so we'll save that topic for a later discussion. You mentioned Post Traumatic Stress. What makes you think you might be dealing with that?"

"I don't; Nick does. He's the one who made the mandate and told me it's what I have." He could hear the petulant tone in his voice, daring her to disagree, but he couldn't help himself. His anxiety level was off the charts, and his normal coping mechanism of humor seemed to have fled, leaving him with immature defiance as his only outlet.

Marilyn nodded, smiling in that soothing way she had been since he showed up. "Do you understand the difference in Post-Traumatic Stress Disorder and normal anxiety and depression?" she asked.

"No," he said. Was his lip actually jutting in a pout? Possibly.

"In Post Traumatic Stress, your brain becomes frozen on that one trauma-inducing moment. Not only do you keep replaying that moment, but you can't break free from the feelings of fear and help-lessness that you may have experienced during that time. The anxiety often manifests itself as vivid nightmares."

Ding! Kelsey shifted uncomfortably when she hit the nail on the head. His dreams were so real he was becoming afraid to close his eyes.

"Often the resulting feelings lead some people to substance abuse as a way of numbing their emotions or trying to find relief."

"There's nothing wrong with enjoying a few drinks," Kelsey replied.

"No, there isn't," Marilyn agreed. "The problem happens when the alcohol begins to take over. Have you experienced any blackouts or memory loss with your drinking lately?"

She pinned him with a stare. *Ding!* Another alarm bell went off as he tried in vain to remember the end of Nick's wedding. It was a complete blank, and that terrified him more than anything else. That he had stripped in a church and called Melly such horrible things was enough to mellow his defiance a little.

"I blacked out at Nick's wedding. I guess I did some pretty awful stuff."

Marilyn nodded, but her placid smile didn't waiver. "It sounds like you're dealing with some guilt and remorse on top of your other emotions. That's not a fun combination. I'm sorry."

He stared at a picture of a dog on the opposite wall, stifling his surprise. She was sorry? Where was the recrimination he deserved? Where was the psychological probing he had been expecting?

"I'm on your side here, Kelsey," Marilyn continued, as if reading his mind. "I can't put myself in your shoes and imagine the things you've seen and experienced because I've never left my safe little world. I've never been a soldier, never watched a friend die, never killed a man. But I do care about my job, and I try very hard to be good at it. I've dealt with a lot of soldiers who have been in situations similar to yours, and not only has it given me a greater respect for what you do, but it has given me a greater understanding and a better ability to help. I would like to help you, but you have to want it. Not for Nick and not to save your job, but because you recognize the fact that, at least for this one moment in time, things are a little overwhelming and you need help."

He scraped his teeth over his bottom lip, continuing to stare at the dog as he considered her words. "What would we do? I don't want to go on a bunch of pills."

"You'll have a say in what we do or don't do. Some men want pills. They want to come in and swallow something that will make their problems go away. To me, that is the greater danger because it means they're treating the symptoms and not the problem. So I'm glad to hear you don't want pills. We'll save those as a last resort. If you agree to keep seeing me, then we'll work on getting your brain unstuck from wherever it is. Something is bothering you. We're going to figure out what it is, and help you move on. There are several ways to do that, and none of them is too painful or scary."

"I know where it's stuck," Kelsey said. "It's stuck on Lolly's death."

"Why?"

"What do you mean why?" he said, becoming angry again. "He was one of my best friends, like a little brother to me, and he died in my arms. Isn't that reason enough?"

"Maybe. But you're a soldier, and I would guess you've seen a lot of death. I also know you're a scout sniper, so it's highly possible that you've caused death. I think it's important for us to discover why Lolly's death is hitting you so hard."

It was the same thing he had thought this morning, but he still found himself rebelling against her. "Because he was like family to me," Kelsey almost yelled. "I loved him. He was my brother."

"Tell me about your biological family," Marilyn said, meeting his anger with a placid calmness that was really starting to annoy him.

"I don't have any," he said.

"None?"

He shook his head. "Maybe some distant cousins somewhere. My parents died when I was four. My grandmother took me in and raised me. She was good to me, and I loved her. She died when I was seventeen."

"So your family died. They abandoned you."

"They didn't abandon me," he yelled. "It wasn't their fault they died."

"I know," Marilyn said. "But do you? Listen to the anger in your voice right now."

He did as she commanded and was surprised by the rage tightening his chest. He had never before realized he was angry with his parents and grandmother for quitting on him, for abandoning him and leaving him to fend for himself. He wasn't sure what to do with the information now.

"But that's not right," he said. "It wasn't their fault."

"Oftentimes our greatest challenge when it comes to mental health is the disconnect between what our rational mind tells us and what our emotions feel," Marilyn said. "Your brain tells you that you shouldn't be angry, that it wasn't their fault they died. But your emotions *are* angry. They want to place blame somewhere."

Kelsey let out a breath and all his energy went with it, leaving him drained and sagging. "I think I might be really messed up."

Marilyn laughed, a light sound that was in stark contrast to the heaviness inside him, but somehow he found himself smiling at her.

"Of course you are not," she said. "You are a man who has been under a great strain and a great amount of responsibility. And now you're continuing to do the right thing by seeking help when you need it and before it's too late."

"So, you don't think it's too late for me? You don't think I'm hopeless?" When had he reverted to being a pathetic little boy who desperately needed approval?

"I don't think anyone is hopeless, or at least that's what I'm supposed to say. But in your case I really mean it. Believe me, Kelsey, I see some real nutters in my job." She smiled, and now it was his turn to laugh.

"Is it Truck? You're talking about Truck, aren't you? You can tell me; I won't say a word." He made a zipping motion across his lips.

"Patient confidentiality," she said. "I would like to meet with you twice a week for the next month, if that's okay with you. Your experience is still fresh, and we have a better possibility of helping you to move on if we strike while the iron is hot."

"As long as you don't actually strike me with a hot iron, then I guess that would be okay," he said.

"We're going to talk, and we're going to give you some homework."

"Homework?" he repeated.

Marilyn nodded. "We're going to try some cognitive dream therapy, basically I will be giving you a script to practice when you wake up from your nightmares, something that will help you find calm so you can go back to sleep. And then we're going to do some eye movement desensitization and reprocessing, or EMDR for short. Are you familiar with that technique?"

He shook his head, worried again by the technical-sounding jargon.

"Basically it means I will be shining a bright light in your eyes while you move them back and forth and we talk through the incident with Lolly. I can't tell you why or how it works, but it has shown great promise in treating Post Traumatic Stress like yours."

"Will there be like hypnotism or electric shock?" Kelsey asked.

"Only if you really want it," she said, and he laughed because she was kidding. He hoped. "Let me reiterate that we're a team. We won't do anything you're uncomfortable with, okay?"

"Okay," he agreed. There was a part of him that realized he had been duped by her. She had sucked him in and played him, allaying his fears by relating to him as a soldier. But there was another part of him that felt hopeful for the first time in a long time. Maybe this woman could actually do what she said; maybe she could help him.

They talked for a few more minutes about innocuous subjects and Kelsey went home. He went to his room, intending to take a short nap and somehow slept for eighteen hours until the nightmares started again and he woke up in a puddle of his own sweat.

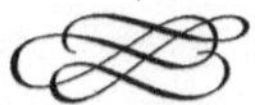

CHAPTER 4

Giving up alcohol was harder than it should have been. Kelsey had never thought of himself as a hard drinker. In high school he had been a partier, like all the other jocks he hung out with. Out of respect for his grandmother, he hadn't been a crazy kid. He had the occasional beer with his friends on the weekends, but he hadn't snuck alcohol into her house or broken any of her other rules. He had even attended church with her every Sunday like the good little boy she wanted him to be.

He joined the marines, and it was a continuation of the party atmosphere, only now instead of doing their hard work on the football field, the work was intensified and spread out, encompassing every aspect of their lives. They worked hard and they partied hard. But again he had been able to compartmentalize. He never drank when he knew he would need a clear head for work; he only drank when it was his weekend, when there was no chance of being called to duty.

Nick's drinking phased out during sniper school, but Kelsey's intensified, just a little. It was a nice break from the pressure of their new job, a pleasant diversion from the cold hard fact that they were being trained to end people's lives. Then Truck was added to their team, and he really had a problem with alcohol. Nick and Kelsey had staged their own sort of intervention, giving him an ultimatum—tone it down, or you're off the team. And Truck had done it, notching down his habit to an occasional beer with supper. Kelsey couldn't remember the last time he had seen his friend drunk, which was both a relief and a little sad because it meant he was now the team drunk. There was the new kid, who drank like a fish, but he also seemed to have an iron stomach, and he wasn't really part of the team yet; he wasn't family. So far, he was some guy they worked and lived with. Kelsey wasn't sure he saw that changing any time soon because the kid wasn't very likeable. Cocky and prickly, he seemed bent on being a problem.

Thankfully for Travis, Kelsey had too many of his own problems to worry about, the chief one being that he had somehow become an alcoholic without even noticing. When? And how? How had he gone from enjoying the occasional drink with a burger to needing one to get through a day? The thought of going without left him feeling panicked, and he didn't like that. He didn't want to admit he had a problem, but the truth was he did. For the first time in his life he was frightened he was going to fail at something because lately all he could think was how very much he wanted a drink.

It was on his mind when he woke in the morning and when he went to bed at night and all the hours in between. If only he could take a few sips of something, then it would ease his progress in therapy. If he could have a glass or four of wine, he could sleep at night without worrying about the nightmares. If he had a few shots in the morning, it would cure the persistent headache he seemed to be carrying around.

Marilyn waited until their sixth therapy session to bring up his drinking and neither of them was prepared for his vehement reaction. "I'm not an alcoholic," he raged.

"I didn't say you were," Marilyn said and then she looked at him with that penetrating gaze he was becoming to recognize, as if waiting for him to catch up with her assessment. And when he did, he was shocked. She *hadn't* said he was an alcoholic. She had simply asked him how much he drank on a daily basis, and he had exploded. Which meant he was touchy about booze, and when had that happened? If it wasn't a problem for him, why was he so touchy?

"I think maybe I am an alcoholic," he said, his tone so repentant and humble Marilyn laughed.

"That was the easiest turnabout I've ever had. You're cured. Go home." She made a waving motion toward the door, and he smiled. His trust and comfort with her had grown exponentially over the last few weeks because he learned she actually cared about him and wasn't out to get him. Or change him. Or have him thrown out of the marines.

It was the day for bombshell topics apparently, because after they spent an inordinate amount of time talking about his growing dependence on alcohol, she mentioned Melly.

"Let's talk about Lolly's sister," Marilyn said, her casual tone in no way indicating she had probably been gunning for this subject for the last couple of weeks.

"What's to discuss?" Kelsey replied. "She's his sister. She's a friend."

"Correct me if I'm wrong, but there seems to be a lot of tension in your voice when you mention her," Marilyn said. She shifted, tipping her face to the side as she studied him. She was a pudgy middle-aged woman whose presence was soothing. It was like having a conversation with someone's mom. Not his mom because she was eternally young in his mind. Not Nick's Mom because she was crazy. Maybe Ashleigh's mom. Yes, Marilyn was a bit reminiscent of Mrs. Desmond.

"We've had our moments over the years. We don't always get along."

"Hmm," Marilyn said.

"Hmm, what?" Kelsey asked.

"I'm not picking up any anger. The sound is similar to when you were talking about giving up alcohol. There's anxiety. Fear."

"Fear?" Kelsey repeated. "Why would I be afraid of Melly?"

"I don't know. Is there a reason? Are you afraid of her?"

His knee-jerk reaction was to say *Of course not. Don't be ridiculous.* But she had him thinking about everything before he answered now.

"I don't know," he said slowly. "Why would I be afraid of Melly?" he asked, meaning the question this time.

"The people you love have a way of abandoning you. Do you think it's possible there's a part of you that's afraid she'll do the same?"

"That would suggest I love her," Kelsey said.

"Don't you? There are all kinds of love, not all of them romantic. If she is your friend, then you must love her."

He nodded. "When you put it like that, it feels okay. Yes, I love her."

"Are you in love with her?" Marilyn pressed.

Kelsey let out a breath. "You're not making this easy."

She smiled. "Not my job to make things easy."

"I don't know what I feel for Melly," he said at last. "Everything is all jumbled up where she's concerned—fear, friendship, guilt."

"Guilt. Let's talk about that," Marilyn said. "Why do you feel guilt?"

"Isn't it obvious? Because I failed. She asked me to keep Lolly safe, to bring him home again, and I failed. I'm a marine, a scout sniper, and I couldn't keep one little innocent guy from being killed. He was all the family she has in the world, and now she's alone."

"She's not alone; she has you."

"Yeah, some prize I am. A crazy, alcoholic failure who can't keep it together, a guy who calls her names and abandons her. Her saint of a brother is gone, and I'm still here. Lucky Melly."

"Do you think when she asked you to keep her brother safe, she meant it?" Marilyn said.

"Of course she did. Lolly was small and innocent."

"But he was a marine, the same as you are. And he was your point man. Aren't they out in front? Statistically speaking, aren't they in a more danger than everyone else?"

"Yes," Kelsey said.

"So don't you think it's possible she knew exactly what her brother was capable of as a marine?"

"I suppose," Kelsey said. "He was very good at reconnaissance, like a ghost."

"Did it ever occur to you she might have said the same thing to him about you? That she might have asked him to take care of you," Marilyn suggested.

Kelsey's mouth opened, but he didn't have a reply. He imagined Melly taking Lolly aside and whispering in his ear. *Take care of Kelsey, Jesus. Bring him back alive.* And it would have been a Melly thing to do, to make them swear to take care of each other by making it seem like one was in charge of the other's safety.

"And do you think if Lolly had failed to do so, if you had died, that Melly would blame her brother for your death?"

"No," Kelsey said. "She would never blame Lolly because it wouldn't be his fault."

She gave him the look again, the one that meant she was waiting for him to catch up with her assessment. He got it, but he didn't admit it. Of course Melly would never blame Lolly, like she didn't blame Kelsey for Lolly's death. He blamed himself, though, and how could he ever get over that?

He was wiped, totally drained from their session, and Marilyn knew it. "I think we're making some good progress, Kelsey," she said, ever the encourager.

"If you say so," he replied. Sensing their session was at a close, he reached into his pocket to turn his phone on, and was immediately surprised when it rang. "It's Truck," he said. Truck wasn't one to call to chat, which meant it must have been important. He pulled out his phone and answered. "What's up?"

"We've got a problem," Truck said.

Kelsey felt an odd sense of relief at his words because he thought they meant they had been called up for an assignment sooner than they were expecting. Escaping the country and Marilyn to focus on work was a much-welcomed distraction at this point. "Yeah?" he said, his tone tinged with suppressed excitement. *Please let us go somewhere far and active so I have no time to think.*

"Shelby called. She was freaking out. Melly's gone."

Kelsey's expectant elation fled as he clutched the phone so tightly he was in danger of snapping it. "What are you saying?"

"I'm saying that Melly's missing, man. She's gone."

He shot to his feet, turning to stare at the dog picture on the far wall. "What do you mean she's gone?"

"I mean gone. Her car is here. Her purse, her phone. And she's gone."

"How long has she been gone?"

"Shelby saw her yesterday morning and then we didn't get home until late last night. Melly's car was here, so Shelby figured she was in her room. But then she came home today and knocked on her door, and Melly's not there. There's no note, no sign of a struggle. Nothing. Gone."

"Stop saying gone," Kelsey said. "She's not gone—she can't be. I'm coming over, and I'll find her." He put away his phone and stared at Marilyn.

"Everything okay?" she asked, obviously knowing that the answer was a resounding no.

"I have to go," Kelsey said. "Melly is missing."

"Can I do anything? Should I call the police?" Marilyn asked.

"No, I have to check things out first, see what the situation is." He headed toward the door and paused, looking back. He wanted to ask her what the chances were of being rescued from the deep end, because if something happened to Melly, he would lose it for sure. He didn't ask the question, though. Instead he gave Marilyn a nod and let himself out, sprinting to his car, his mind in a panicked blur.

He was the last one to arrive at Melly's house. Shelby, Truck, Nick, Ashleigh, even the Desmonds and Travis were there before him which made him angry because it meant they had tried to handle it without involving him, only calling him in when it was apparent Melly was really gone.

"What happened?" he asked Shelby.

"I saw her at breakfast yesterday morning."

"How did she seem?" Kelsey interrupted.

"Normal. Calm. Contained. She went to work, I know because I checked. And then I don't know what happened. Her car was here. I thought she was. Ashton and I went out for supper and I didn't see her, but she spends a lot of time in her room." She paused, biting her lip. "Sometimes I hear her crying, and then when I see her she pretends she wasn't. She's private with her emotions. So I thought maybe she was crying or napping and I didn't want to interrupt. We left and came home after eleven. Melly is always in bed by ten, so I didn't think to check on her. She didn't come out this morning, but I didn't think anything of it. Ashton and I spent the day hiking and came back here for supper. I didn't want to invade her space, but I was uncomfortable at not having seen her in so long, so I knocked on the door and there was no answer. I opened it, and the bed was made. The room looked untouched. I tried calling her phone and found that it was in her purse on the counter." She sniffled and wiped her eyes. Truck stepped forward and slid his arm around her waist.

Kelsey wanted to rail at her, to ask why she hadn't pressed harder or noticed Melly's absence before. But he couldn't, not least of which because Truck would rip his arms off and make him eat them. It wasn't her fault, though. Shelby was right; Melly was self-contained. It wouldn't have been unusual for her to closet herself in her room for long periods of time. He should be thanking Shelby for checking on her when she did, and so he did.

"Thanks for checking on her, for looking out for her."

"Y-you're welcome," she said, blinking up at him in confusion.

"Do you have any idea where she might be?"

Shelby shook her head. "I tried her boyfriend's number, but he hasn't heard from her."

"Her boyfriend," Kelsey repeated, clutching his hands into fists at his side.

Shelby nodded, looking apprehensive again. "Robert. You met him at the wedding."

"I didn't know that was her boyfriend," Kelsey said. She had a boyfriend when she kissed him? How very un-Melly.

"They were only friends then. She, uh, was having a difficult time there for a while, and he helped her through. They've become an item the last few weeks."

"Where is he? I want him here now." Kelsey said, he looked around, scanning the circle to find a target for his impotent rage. "You," he pointed at Travis. "Go and find this guy and bring him here."

"He's at the hospital," Ashleigh said, sounding exasperated.

"Is he sick?" Kelsey asked.

"No, he's a pediatrician and he's on call this weekend. Melly wasn't planning to see him because he'll basically be living at the hospital until Monday," Ashleigh said. "Kelsey, we understand your anger, but Robert's the wrong target. The man's a saint."

Unlike you. The unspoken words hung between them and Nick stepped forward. "We'll check with Robert, okay? Make sure he understands the situation and knows nothing that might help. Shelby, Truck, why don't you go talk to him, impress upon him the need for total disclosure."

"What can we do?" Caleigh asked. She stepped up and stood beside Travis. When had that happened? Were they actually a couple now? Kelsey hoped not. Nick, too, if the frown on his face was any indication.

"You guys start calling hospitals and the police. We can't file a missing person's report yet, but we can get Melly's name and description on their radar so they'll keep an eye out. Ash and I will go talk to the neighbors, see if they saw or heard anything suspicious. Mom and Dad, can you find the name of her principal? Give her a call and ask questions about Melly, if she's been having any trouble lately, that sort of thing."

Nick was freakishly good at taking charge, but right now Kelsey resented it. Melly was his responsibility; he should be calling the shots. "What about me, Obi Wan?" he asked.

"You search her room, see what you can come up with. No one has touched it yet because we didn't want to invade, but if anyone can find anything that doesn't belong, it's you." Nick clapped him on the shoulder, undeterred by his bad attitude, and Kelsey clapped his back in return as he passed—their version of an apology.

Stepping into Melly's bedroom felt like stepping into the inner sanctum, a feeling that wasn't helped by how freakishly tidy everything was. "Geez, Melly," he whispered. "Would it hurt you to leave a gum wrapper or two lying about?" Not one item was out of place, but that was Melly—a neat, driven perfectionist. The woman never even broke the speed limit and yet still arrived everywhere with five minutes to spare. She was punctual, committed, loyal, and there was no way she should be missing without a really good reason. Kelsey's hands shook and he took a steadying breath, holding off that line of thought for the time being. It was still entirely possible Melly had gone somewhere and forgotten to tell anyone, like it was entirely possible he would find her appointment book and it would say "Saturday eight AM: Disappear and freak everyone out." Right. Likely.

He surveyed the room, not knowing where to start. Someone had moved her purse into the room and set it on her bed, so he started there. He opened the purse and stuck his head inside, catching a heart-wrenching whiff of Melly's scent. He closed his eyes and tried to block it out because it conjured everything about her, from her annoyingly straight-laced demeanor to her overly passionate kissing style. Melly was a maddening study in contrasts. When Kelsey thought he had her pegged as a square, buttoned-down goody two shoes, she grabbed him and kissed those thoughts away. And when he started to believe she had finally taken down her barriers and turned into the firecracker of his dreams, she shoved him away and returned to her boyfriend, Robert-the-superhero pediatrician. How fitting that Melly, a kindergarten teacher who adored children, should fall for the world's most boring and ordinary pediatrician. They deserved each other, and Kelsey wished them every happiness. He wanted to kill the other man, to literally rip his head from his body, but that was a normal reaction when one of your friends began dating someone. Wasn't it? He would have to ask Marilyn.

He dumped the contents of Melly's purse on the bed and began to sort through them, but there wasn't much. Her phone was there. He set it aside for later inspection. Her wallet was there, and he rifled through it. Her credit card and driver's license were there. The wallet was empty of money, but so was his because he preferred to use plastic. There was a makeup pouch, a pen, and pad of paper. He flipped through the pad of paper, but only one page had been written on, and it contained a grocery list. He paused, his heart beating faster when he saw his own name. "Kelsey—birthday card?" Since his birthday was coming up in a couple of weeks, he could only assume Melly had been trying to decide if she should buy him a card. Knowing her, she probably would, and then she would sign it with her name and nothing else and he would track her down, outraged by the impersonal lack of a greeting when in years past she had written him cards with funny poems on them.

"Roses are red, violets are blue, today is your birthday, I'm bad at rhyming," being his favorite from two years ago. He smiled as he reached for her phone and his heart caught again because a picture of Melly and Lolly came to life and jumped out at him. He looked at it a minute, a wave of sadness and grief washing over him at the loss of both of them. Somehow over the last three years, they had become so much a part of him he truly thought of them as family. Now Lolly was gone and he had shoved Melly away, and he was feeling their loss keenly.

He scrolled through her calls and found five to his own number, all canceled almost as soon as they were sent, as if she had dialed and then changed her mind. "Ah, Melly," he whispered, hating the fact that she had apparently been twisting up in knots over him. Why couldn't she forget him and move on? Enjoy life with Robert-the-magnificent. Though maybe she had if the massive amount of calls to and from Robert's number were any indication. Either they were so in love they couldn't stay off the phone, or they saw each other so rarely a phone connection was all they had. Whatever the reason, they spent a lot of time talking.

What did they talk about? Kelsey wondered. Did they talk about him? Lolly? Their jobs? Their pasts? For that matter, what did he and Melly ever talk about? They argued, bickered, and flirted, but they only rarely talked. She was a private person who didn't like to talk about her feelings and thoughts. More often than not it was him doing the talking, and he had opened up to her more than he had ever opened up to anyone. There had been nights when she had stayed at their house and stayed awake with him all night, probing into his psyche, trying to get him to hash out his issues the way she did to Lolly. She was always concerned over their mental health, knowing how much they had to deal with on the job. And she wasn't nosy about it, either, which he appreciated. Some girls he dated felt they had a right to know the details of his assignments. They would probe around and ask detailed questions, taking his lack of a response as a sign of his distrust in them. Melly knew better. She never asked where they went or what they had done. She simply asked how it went and how they were feeling.

He and Lolly had joked that Melly should be charging them for her forced therapy sessions, but now that he was actually in therapy he knew it wasn't the same. He and Marilyn never lay on the living room floor together, the television playing quietly in the background as he ran his fingers through her hair and poured out his heart. That was what Melly was for, though the result was the same: Kelsey felt better. She was the only woman he had ever spent an entire night with, talk-ing. She was the only woman he was himself with, the only woman he could turn off the flirting, funny portion of himself and be Kelsey. And, wonder of wonders, she seemed to prefer him that way. He knew because she had told him once. *Want to know a secret, Kelsey?* she had asked, grabbing his hand and twining her fingers through his. *I like you better this way.* He had just returned from a particularly long and grueling assignment, and he hadn't had the emotional energy to deal with whatever it was she might have been saying. So he had grabbed her and pulled her close, burying his face in her neck.

How much better? he had asked, and she had kneed him in the stomach as she struggled to get away from his oppressive clutch. That had been his M/O for most of their relationship, advance, retreat, advance, retreat. Make an emotional connection, ruin it with a joke and pull back. Melly had never complained because she seemed to be doing the same sort of dance, as if she were as afraid of him as he was of her. Why, though? He had never asked himself that question before, assuming Melly simply didn't trust him because she knew he was a player. But was that really it, or did Melly have her own reasons for keeping an emotional barrier between them?

Why had he never asked her? Why had he been content to take and take from her without ever giving back? He was a part of her life to a certain extent. He knew the names of her coworkers and friends, knew what she did for a living, knew her frustrations as a kindergarten teacher, knew she had adored Lolly. But that was it. What motivated her to be the overachiever she was? How did she feel when her family died and she was left to raise Lolly alone while still a kid herself? How did she manage all those years before he started basic training? How did she feel about moving across the country to follow her brother when he was stationed in North Carolina? How did she feel about her Mexican heritage? Why did she keep herself closed off from everyone around her?

Kelsey pulled himself from his torturous recrimination and made himself focus on her phone. All of the calls were numbers he recognized. Ashleigh, Shelby, Mrs. Desmond, and even Caleigh were included in her call list. Since Lolly's death, Melly had become especially close to Ashleigh's family and her church, which surprised him. Lolly had been a dyed-in-the-wool Catholic; he couldn't believe Melly had turned protestant. But maybe it was a sign of how desperate she had been for support because the church *had* been supportive, showering her with cards, food, and phone calls. He would say this for Ashleigh's church: they were good at taking care of people. Much better than he was, apparently.

He set Melly's purse aside with a disgusted shove. Time to move on to something else. He stood and began carefully rifling through her drawers, resisting the urge to whistle in wonder over her underpants. His little Melly wasn't such a schoolmarm when it came to her lingerie, something he definitely planned to tease her about when he saw her again. He wouldn't allow himself to think "if" he saw her again because he would. He wasn't one to take no for an answer, and this was no exception.

There was nothing significant in her drawers, besides the fact that she could have been a professional clothes sorter and folder. He moved on to the closet, but it was more of the same—clothes arranged by season, color, sleeve length. Her shoes were no different, lined up at perfect right angles by season, color, and type.

A box at the top of the closet caught his eye because it looked like a girl box, a place to store treasures and memories. Of course, knowing Melly, it could have been her tax returns because she wasn't exactly the sentimental type. But when he pulled it down and opened it his first instinct had been correct because it was a box of memories.

Kelsey sat on the bed again and began sorting. The first thing he saw was a stack of pictures of Melly. One was a snapshot of her in the hospital, and the rest were school and professional pictures arranged in order until around age nine. She was a pretty girl, her little Melly smile firmly in place. Her clothes were nicer than he would have imagined immigrants could provide. Maybe her parents had spent all their money trying to dress her and Lolly like American children. Kelsey didn't know. *Because you never asked,* he reminded himself, grimacing over his selfishness.

There were other pictures in the box, pictures of Lolly, of Ashleigh, himself, and two of Robert. Kelsey paused, fighting the urge to rip them in half. The pictures were of the couple together, Robert's arm around Melly's waist as they squinted and smiled into the camera. They appeared to be hiking somewhere. He shuffled those pictures to the back of the stack and inspected the photo of himself with her. It had been taken a couple of years ago at a baseball game. For some reason Truck hadn't been able to go, so Melly had made up their fourth, and it had been a lot of fun. She and Kelsey had miraculously spent the day argument free, and Lolly had taken their picture to commemorate the event.

"Pose like you're in love," Lolly had commanded, and so they had, laying it on thick as they snuggled up to each other like two teenagers on their first date. Melly had even called him "Snooky-wookems," so he was laughing right as the picture was snapped. They looked happy and, sure enough, in love.

The next picture was one he had never seen before and he only vaguely remembered it. He and Melly were on the beach, walking hand in hand as they appeared to be deep in conversation. Lolly must have snapped it for whatever reason when they weren't looking, and the candid photo made Kelsey's breath catch because it somehow revealed the depth of his friendship with Melly. He probably hadn't even known he was holding on to her as they walked and talked because they didn't normally hold hands. His mouth was open, his brows down as if he were discussing a serious topic. Melly, on the other hand, had her face tipped up in his direction, a slight smile playing on her lips. Whatever he was saying, she seemed to be laughing at him, at least a little bit, and he smiled. She never let him take himself too seriously, never let his head get too big.

Kelsey put the pictures away and sorted the other contents of the box. There were cards, some from Lolly, a couple written in Spanish that may have been from her mother. There were two from Robert and they both ended with the "L" word. Kelsey was irrationally angry the unknown man had already told her he loved her. He hadn't been vetted yet; he was not allowed to be moving that quickly.

There were none from him, most likely because he hadn't given her any. He usually texted or called her on her birthday, and now he was rethinking that strategy. Cards were nice; cards could be kept in a box, giving the sender special status like give-the-woman-some-space Robert.

"Melly, where are you?" Kelsey whispered. He put the box away, got down on his hands and knees, and searched under her bed. It was immaculate, not even a dust bunny dared to dwell there. The last place to look was her nightstand and he frowned at it, not wanting to know what he might find. But when he tried to open the drawer, he realized with some relief it was a false front. A small basket beside the bed held a bottle of hand lotion and a tube of lip balm, and that was it; the room was done. He sat on the bed again, scanning for anything he might have missed, but there was nothing. The room was as straight-forward as Melly with no dark secrets to hide. For the first time in a long time, he felt the urge to pray, to reach up to some supreme being who might be looking down and could take care of Melly.

He felt too foolish to form the words, so he merely sent up a thought. *Help me find her, please,* and then a knock sounded on the door. For one wild second, he expected it to be Melly with an angel beam on her head and the booming message "I told you I was real" echoing around the room. But it wasn't Melly; it was Truck.

"Robert's here," he said. "And he wants to see you."

Kelsey cast his eyes heavenward. "Thanks a lot," he muttered, then he left the room and closed the door.

CHAPTER 5

Robert was waiting in the living room, his arms stiff at his sides as if preparing himself for something unpleasant. Since Kelsey could literally dismantle the smaller man with his bare hands, he hoped he wasn't preparing himself to take a swing. On a good day, Kelsey would dodge the blow and laugh about it. Today he might let it land and retaliate. Like usual Nick read his mind, cleared his throat, and shook his head.

Kelsey stood down and clasped his arms behind his back, a conscious reminder to himself he was a marine and his team leader was present. "What can I do for you Dr. Bob?"

"I want to know where Melly is," Robert said.

"So do I," Kelsey replied. "Do you have any idea?"

"No, but you do."

Kelsey scowled down at him. Maybe it was shallow, but he was enjoying the height advantage. "What are you talking about? Why would I know where Melly is?"

"Because she told me that sometimes she wanted to run away but it would be useless because you would know how to find her."

Kelsey was so startled by that unexpected pronouncement he looked down to see if he had taken a step back. He was still rooted to the same spot, so he must be only mentally ajar. "Why would she say that?"

"You tell me. What do you know about her that could help you find her?"

Kelsey shook his head. "Nothing. There's nothing."

"There must be something," Robert pressed. "Think."

Kelsey pressed his hands to his temples. "You know what doesn't help you think? Someone shouting at you to think. Shut up a minute." Why would Melly say he could find her? Was it because he was trained in recon? Because he had a stubborn, indomitable personality that didn't believe in taking no for an answer? Or was it something she had told him that he was now supposed to remember? "I don't know," he said at last. "Has she said anything to you? Was she in trouble of any kind?"

"Melly?" Robert repeated. "How could Melly possibly be in trouble?"

"Did she mention anything or not?" Kelsey snapped.

"No. There was nothing, unless you count the wedding where you humiliated her. There were a couple of bad days after that, but she's been fine since then."

Kelsey winced, which was probably the guy's intention, but he couldn't reply because he had it coming. If Melly had gone somewhere of her own free will, how could she have slipped away without a word to anyone? And if she hadn't gone of her own free will, then why was there no sign of a struggle or forced entry? Had she gone with someone she knew? But who did she know besides them?

"Did anyone find out anything today?" Kelsey asked, scanning the room.

"None of the neighbors saw anything," Nick volunteered.

"Her principal said she wasn't having any problems at work," Mrs. Desmond added.

"Nothing with the police or hospitals," Caleigh said.

"I think it's time to call in the media," Robert said.

Everyone turned to him and looked to Kelsey for his reaction. Kelsey thought it over, trying to decide what his gut was telling him, what his instinct suggested. "I think it's too soon for that," he said at last, hoping he was right.

"Frankly, I don't care what you think," Robert said. "This is about Melly."

"Yes, it is," Kelsey agreed. "And if you know Melly at all then you'll know she would be humiliated by the public attention if she's slipped away somewhere to think."

"Why would she do that without telling us anything? She knows we would worry."

"Maybe not," Kelsey said. "Melly withdraws when she's hurting or upset over something. It's possible she's withdrawn so much she doesn't realize how worried we are." He hadn't realized he knew that about her until he said it, and then he realized it was true. He wondered what else his subconscious had picked up about the woman he considered his closest female friend. Hopefully it was something that would help him find her.

"I think this is a mistake," Robert said. "I think we need a media blitz with her picture everywhere until we find her."

"No," Kelsey said. Robert opened his mouth to argue, but Kelsey held up his hand. "Give us until tomorrow to try and locate her."

Robert pointed his finger at Kelsey's chest. "If you're wrong and something has happened to her, then it's on your shoulders."

"I absolve you of all responsibility," Kelsey said. "And since you've been absolved, why don't you run along home and try to think of anything that might help because you standing there trying to be macho doesn't." He didn't wait to see if Robert obeyed his order. Instead he turned and went back to Melly's room, perching once again on the edge of her bed.

By nature, Kelsey wasn't a thinker; he was a man of action. On assignment, Nick and Truck were always the ones urging caution and forethought while Kelsey was the one always saying, "Enough talking, let's go!" But now he felt the need to think, and the best place to do that was in Melly's bedroom where it was quiet and smelled like her. Maybe being surrounded by her scent would help him think like her.

Overcome by curiosity, he pulled back her comforter and peeked at her sheets, chuckling at what he saw. On the outside, her bed was an innocuous white duvet. Underneath, her sheets were dusky purple and satin. It wasn't a difficult leap to say the bed was a metaphor for its owner: prim and proper on the outside, a passionate firebrand underneath.

He tugged off his shoes and crawled between the sheets, staring at the ceiling. What had Melly thought when she lay here? What had she thought on the night of Lolly's funeral? Had she wished for him the same way he had wished for her? Had she understood he stayed away as a form of self-punishment?

There was something tickling the back of his brain, something about Melly, but what?

A knock on the door interrupted his thoughts. Nick and Ashleigh entered. It was a testament to their close friendship that they showed no reaction to the sight of him tucked up in Melly's frilly purple sheets.

"Time for my night-night story?" he asked when they sat on either side of him.

"We're going for food and then a bunch of us are going to meet at the church to make some flyers and strategize for tomorrow's search. Can I bring you anything? Coffee? Cocoa? *Goodnight Moon?*" Nick said.

He smiled and closed his eyes. "My mom used to read me that book."

"It's a great book," Ashleigh said. She rested her hand on his forearm and gave it a squeeze. "We're going to find her."

"I know," Kelsey said, not doubting it for a second. If he had to tear the state of North Carolina apart with his bare hands, then he would do it. "It's that when we do, I have an awful lot to make up for." He opened his eyes, staring at the ceiling once again.

"What will Melly say when you have this conversation with her?" Ashleigh asked. She was a few years younger than him, but also very motherly which made for an odd combination. Despite the fact that she was pretty, Kelsey had never been attracted to her, but Nick certainly was, which was a good thing since he was the one who married her.

"She'll tell me I'm the world's biggest jerk, and then she'll forgive me," Kelsey said. "But it's not Melly's forgiveness that's hard to accept —it's mine." He could tell he had surprised them with his bald admission, which meant it was time to make a joke. He sat up and looked around in confusion. "Marilyn? I had this dream where I was having a therapy session and you were there, and you." He pointed at them, and they smiled.

"We'll always be there," Nick said, ruining the joke with his sincere and caring tone.

"I know." Kelsey sighed and flopped back onto the sheets. "Now get out of here, you two, so I can try to pretend I hate the feel of satin against my cheek. If you hear anything, call me, okay? I think I'm going to bunk down here for the night in case I think of something or in case Melly comes home."

"That works both ways. If you think of anything or if Melly comes home, then give us a call, no matter what time."

"Sir, yes sir," Kelsey said. His eyes drifted closed because satin really was enjoyable on his cheek and the emotionally draining day was catching up with him. With Melly gone, he was sure he wouldn't be able to sleep, but by the time Nick and Ashleigh tiptoed from the room, he was snoring.

CHAPTER 6

*K*elsey was dreaming. Not his normal dream, the one where Lolly was shot and he couldn't carry him, couldn't make it to the helicopter. This one was different because it was about Melly, but it was no less intense. She was running and he was chasing, only she was afraid of him and kept turning to look over her shoulder.

"I'm trying to help you," he called. "Stop."

But she didn't stop, didn't slow down, didn't respond. She simply kept running and running, and then she was gone. He jumped and woke up, drenched in sweat as had become his nightly routine. His anxiety was intense, making it hard to swallow, and he practiced the calming technique Marilyn had showed him by imagining himself in full gear in a room with Nick and Truck, their weapons at the ready. They were about to go into a battle of some sort, but it was okay because they would succeed. He was smiling, and so were his friends. It probably said something about the state of his psyche that his happy place was in full battle dress, holding a gun, but that was where he felt most secure because he was in control.

The imagery began to work its magic, and Kelsey's hitched breathing returned to normal. He was safe; he was in Melly's bedroom. But where was Melly? The dream had triggered something, some latent thought he couldn't reach, but what was it?

The pictures of her as a little girl sprang to mind and he gave them a mental review, shifting through each one in his imagination, trying to figure out what about them was bothering him. At last he gave up on his mental recall and sat up, turning on the bedside lamp. It was dawn, but not light enough to make his way in the unfamiliar room. He reached for the box at the top of the closet and pulled it down, crawling back under the covers to look at the contents.

He bypassed the letters and picked up the pictures, laying them on the bed in order of age. There was nothing remarkable about the pictures, except maybe the quality. Photos of him as a child were often grainy or blurry as if his parents hadn't been able to afford a camera with enough pixels to take a quality picture. The before school snap-shots of Melly, however, were remarkably clear and high quality. Her clothes looked expensive, too, except for the one where she was wearing a t-shirt with a picture of a cartoon character on it. Kelsey set that one aside before snatching it up again and holding it close to his face. He tilted it to the right to catch the light better. How could the little girl version of Melly be wearing a picture of a cartoon character that had only been created five years ago? Obviously the pictures weren't of Melly, but who were they? And why did she look exactly like Melly, right down to the dimples in her cheeks?

Kelsey sorted through them again, focusing this time on the picture of the baby. The baby was being held by someone, someone whose hands he now recognized. Melly was holding the newborn in the picture, but why? Was she a cousin? The possibility that the baby might be Melly's came out of nowhere and lingered. No. No way Melly had a baby. She would have told him. Wouldn't she? Or wouldn't Lolly have mentioned it in all the many hours they had spent talking on assignments together? No, this was his overly tired brain leaping at windmills. Of course Melly didn't have a baby; she was the most upstanding person he knew, with the possible exception of Ashleigh. On the other hand it would explain so much about her reserve and the haunted, pained look that occasionally fled her face.

Kelsey had tacked that up to her parents' deaths, but what if it was something else? What if she was a mother?

"Crazy," he whispered, but he couldn't make himself believe it. He was now more desperate than ever to find her and ask her, to make her tell him the truth, to ask her questions he should have asked her years ago during any of their long-winded chat sessions.

His dream had jogged something else loose, too, something about a happy place, but what was it? Something about Melly's happy place. He bolted upright, spilling the photos onto the floor before quickly shoving them back into the box. That was it, the long-ago conversation that had been niggling in the back of his brain. He had once told Melly his happy place was on a warm beach with a beautiful woman and in an uncharacteristic lowering of her guard, she had told him her happy place, too.

My happy place is much more boring. I would go to a hotel. They're anonymous and people take care of you. That's weird, huh? Kelsey had agreed it was weird, and she had laughed, but she had been serious. There were thousands and thousands of hotels all across the country, though. How was he supposed to know which one?

Suddenly the answer was so simple he didn't realize how he hadn't known before. Her car was in the drive, which meant she would have had alternate transportation to wherever she went. No one she knew had given her a ride, which left the option of a taxi. He pulled out his phone and began scrolling through the directory until he located two taxi services. It was early, but he took a chance and called them anyway. One answered and he used his official "marine" voice, the one that sounded full of authority like there might be some sort of legal reason to give him the requested information. Either the guy who answered was too tired to know he didn't owe Kelsey any information or he simply didn't care because he looked up the call and told Kelsey exactly where Melly had gone—a hotel less than ten minutes away.

Kelsey thanked him and put away his phone, deciding to wait until he had Melly in hand before notifying the others. What if the hotel had been her stopping point before going somewhere else? Maybe she hopped a plane or train or went somewhere else. If she was really having some sort of breakdown, then her behavior would be unpredictable.

He gathered his shoes and tiptoed out of the house, noting as he went that Shelby and Truck had fallen asleep on the couch together, cuddled together like two halves of a clamshell, his arms wrapped protectively around her, cocooning. Shelby had her phone in one hand and a flyer of Melly in the other. By the swollen set of her eyes and her little shuddering breaths, Kelsey wondered if she had been crying. Maybe Melly's disappearance brought up her own kidnapping and subsequent horror.

He drove to the hotel and was thankful to see the person on duty was a young woman. If it had been a man, then he would have had less hope of getting the number of Melly's room. As it was, he had a good chance of cajoling the woman into compliance because he had a way with women. Not Melly, but most women.

"Hey," he said as he approached, giving her his most self-deprecating smile. "I know this is totally against policy and you're probably going to say no, but I had this horrible fight with my girlfriend, and she came here to get away from me. I'm a total jerk, but if I don't find her, then I can't apologize and I really, really want to apologize. She's the one, you know? She had me at hello, and all that. Could you help a down-on-his-luck marine and please, please, please tell me her room number?" He clasped his hands together and gave her the puppy dog stare he had perfected in his youth. It didn't work as well with blue-green eyes, but he added in a jutting lip for good measure, and she relaxed.

"What's her name?"

"Mellisandra Garcia. She's about this tall." He held his hand up to his shoulder. "Dark hair, curvy, always thinks she's right. Flaming bad temper."

The woman chuckled. "You're not off to a good start if you're going to talk like that," the woman said.

"Beautiful, curvaceous, smart, funny, adorable, actually always is right," he added, and the woman nodded approvingly.

"Three-twenty-one, but you didn't hear it from me."

"My lips are sealed," he said, making a zipping motion across his mouth.

"For her sake I hope not," the woman said, adding a flirtatious little wink for good measure.

Kelsey laughed his surprise and gave the woman a friendly wave as he walked away. "Thanks," he called. Once he was out of sight of the desk, he took the stairs and sprinted up to the third floor. Now that he was this close to finding her, he was suddenly nervous. What state would she be in? Should he call Marilyn and have her on standby for some sort of psychic break?

But when he knocked on the door, Melly answered, looking as calm, cool, and collected as ever. "Oh, hello," she said.

He stared at her, blinking a few times to make sure she was intact and not hysterical. "Melly, what the crud?"

Melly laughed, a short bark of a sound, and then she dissolved into a fit of weeping, crumpling as she covered her face with her hands. Kelsey had never seen her cry before, not even at Lolly's funeral. She had stood stoic and subdued, holding on to the triangular flag as if it were a lifeline. And now she was sobbing without end. He came inside, closed the door, and put his arms around her. He thought maybe she would resist or struggle, but she didn't. She dissolved into him, sliding her arms around his neck as she pressed her face to his chest.

"*Lo que está mal, mi amor?*" He used the phrase Lolly had reluctantly taught him, the piece of Spanish he pulled out when Melly was angry with him and he wanted to irritate her further by asking her what was wrong, only now he said it softly, tenderly, and she wept harder, shaking her head against his chest.

He picked her up and sat in the ugly armchair by the bed, cradling Melly as if she were a child, and she responded in kind, shuddering violently with her tears. He wondered how long it had been since she cried. Maybe this release had been building for years.

"*Está bien*, Melly," he tried again.

To his surprise, she spoke, though it was in Spanish, so he didn't catch much of it. "No, Kelsey, *no todo está bien. Todo está mal.*" She blinked up at him. "*Tu ternura me encanta.*" She pressed her palm to his cheek and attempted a watery smile.

"So this is what you do in your happy place? You cry? Cause, I gotta tell you, Melly, that sort of takes away from the happy portion of things," he said.

"Better than your shallow vision of a happy place, making out with someone whose bra size is bigger than her IQ."

"That was my old happy place. You haven't heard the new one."

"Reading Dickens by the fire?" she guessed.

He smiled. "You know me too well, although it was Chaucer. So what's up?"

"Nothing," she said, beginning to close her emotional walls again.

"Clearly," he said. "Because I often disappear and go to hotels to cry. That's a totally normal thing to do."

"I needed a couple of days away to think," she said. "I haven't been crying the whole time. I haven't cried at all until now."

"Why didn't you tell someone you were going?" he said.

"I didn't think anyone would notice."

He wanted to shake her because she hadn't meant it in a "Poor me, nobody notices Melly so I'd better get some attention" kind of way. She truly believed no one would notice that she vanished into thin air. "Shelby was crying. She thinks you were kidnapped. The church spent the evening making up a thousand flyers to hand out on street corners today, and your boyfriend wanted to call CNN."

She flinched. "You didn't let him, did you?"

"No."

She fidgeted with the collar of his shirt, staring at it. "What did you do?"

"I spent the night in your bed. Nice sheets, by the way." Before she could take the time to become outraged over his invasion, he decided to make it worse. "I also rifled through your things in an attempt to figure out where you might have gone."

"You went through my things?" she said, sitting up slightly to move away from him.

"Every single one of them, and may I say kudos on your choice of underpants? Really, hats off to you, Miss I-pretend-to-wear-cotton-briefs." He used his hand on her back to tug lightly on her pants and was rewarded with a blush.

"Kelsey," she said, shoving at his chest. "You had no right to rifle my drawers."

"Of course I did when you do something as stupid as run away. I didn't have the right to enjoy it so much, but I couldn't help myself. Now tell me why you're here."

"I already told you. I needed some space to think."

"About what?"

"You wouldn't understand," she said, but she sank against his chest once again. She closed her eyes and pressed her face to his shirt, inhaling.

"Are you sniffing me?" he asked.

"Yes."

"Why?"

"Because I like the way you smell," she said.

"With a compliment like that, aren't you afraid I'm going to get a big head?" he asked.

"No, because it is physically impossible for your ego to get any larger. You're beautiful, smell amazing, and you know it. I could stare at you and sniff you all day, and I might as well enjoy the portions of you that are easy to enjoy."

"If that's our new philosophy, life is about to get a lot more fun," he said.

She smiled and opened her eyes. "Maybe it should be. Maybe I should self-destruct because what does it really matter anymore?"

"Melly, we're not leaving this chair until you tell me what's going on. Is this about Lolly?"

"No. Just go. I'm fine." She tried to squirm away, but he pinned her to him.

"Is it about your daughter?"

She froze, a look of absolute horror creeping over her face. Kelsey was afraid his face might reflect the same expression because he had been firing blanks, not really believing it was the case. He expected her to shove him again and tell him he was crazy for thinking such a thing. Instead she whispered, "How did you know?"

"The pictures. She looks exactly like you. I thought it was you at first. I still can't quite believe it's not."

She pressed her lips together and looked away. "Yeah, well now you know."

It was all there in those five words, her lingering shame, embarrassment, and defiance. As if she thought he was going to dump her on the floor and flee the room in disgust. "No, I don't know because you haven't told me. Why don't you start from the beginning and fill me in?" The hand on her back began rubbing in a small, soothing circle and she melted a little, turning to look at him, her wide chocolate eyes filled with wonder over his seeming acceptance. "Please," he added. "I really want to know about her."

"It's a long story," she said. She sounded so weary and broken that he cupped her face and made her look at him.

"Please, Melly. It would mean a lot to me if you would confide in me."

She blinked at him again as if she couldn't quite believe his new, caring attitude. "My parents came to this country from Mexico when my mother was pregnant with me. They were illegal, brought here by a coyote who worked for a group of rich whites looking for cheap labor. We were lucky because it could have been so much worse than it was. Both my parents were hired by the same family—my father as the gardener, and my mother as the housekeeper. They even let her bring me along while she worked, as long as she got her work done and kept me quiet. We didn't have much, but we made do. My parents were frugal and put a lot of money into savings, not quite trusting that they wouldn't be discovered and tossed out of the country at any time.

"Jesus was born when I was four. They wanted other children, but we were all they got. We were a very close family until they died. I was seventeen, Jesus was thirteen, and I was terrified we were going to be split up. But then a miracle happened: our parents' employer took us in. They had always been kind to us, giving us their hand-me-downs and buying us new things. They treated us like family, but I never dreamed they would go to such an extent to take care of us. It was a very hard time, but made easier by their kindness.

"Then, a few weeks after we moved in with them, the husband began taking special interest in me. He was a kind, charming, and handsome man. It was innocent at first, sort of a fatherly concern. By the time it progressed to something more, I fancied myself in love with him. His wife was at times distant and cold, or so he told me. I convinced myself that this made everything okay because he needed me.

"I was so innocent. I barely had any idea how babies were made, let alone how to use birth control. And then I found out I was pregnant. You have to understand I had been such a good girl to this point. Driven, disciplined, quiet. I had never even dated anyone, preferring to focus on my schoolwork instead. I dreamed of college, and I knew the only way to get there was to work as hard as I could with no distractions. And then suddenly I was eighteen and pregnant, living in another woman's house and taking up with her husband. As soon as I saw the test, it was as if the blinders came off and I saw what I had been doing, saw how wrong it was. I didn't even tell him about the baby. I simply packed up Jesus and left.

"After that things were hard for a while. I was old enough to be Jesus's legal guardian, but I had no money, no job, no skills. What little money my parents left was quickly used up trying to survive those first couple of months.

"I was getting big by this point, and I could no longer keep my secret from Jesus. Telling him was the hardest thing I have ever done, but you know what he was like. He responded with love, kindness, and support, and a heavy dose of anger. He demanded to know who the father was, but I wouldn't tell him. He was so small, even smaller back then, and I was afraid he would demand justice from our former friend." She paused, considering. "I think that was one reason he joined the marines, because he felt like he was unable to protect me as he was." She swiped at her eyes before continuing.

"The only option was giving her up for adoption. It wasn't what I wanted. I wanted to keep my baby, but it wasn't possible. I could barely provide for Jesus. What kind of life would she have living in the slums with an unwed teenage mother? So I went through the church and found a nice family. They paid my living expenses during my pregnancy, which was a blessing because I was sick and couldn't work. Instead I focused on delivering a healthy baby for them, reading to her each night, listening to classical music, eating well, and exercising. And then it was over. I had her, spent three hours saying goodbye, and handed her over. They love her, they're good parents, they send me a picture a year. But it still hurts, every minute of every day."

"Ah, Melly," Kelsey said. He pressed his hand over her ear, pulling her closer to his chest. "Why didn't you ever tell me?"

"Why would I? I was so ashamed of what I had done. Not only did I have a baby out of wedlock, but I had an affair with a married man. I'm glad my mother wasn't around to see the way I failed."

"Melly, you were seventeen and the man was a father figure to you. He took advantage of your youth and your grief."

"No. I wasn't a stupid kid. I was smart and mature; I knew better."

"All kids are stupid and think they know better, but that's the thing: they're kids. Look at Caleigh, she's a great kid and yet she's willingly throwing herself at Travis because she thinks it's for the best. And you can't tell her different because she thinks she's a grownup. You did the best you could with what you had to work with at the time. You got out of the situation, and you made the ultimate sacrifice of giving your baby a better life. Don't ever be ashamed of that."

She narrowed her eyes on him. "You're being very nice to me. Why?"

"What do you mean why? You're one of my best friends. Why shouldn't I be nice to you?"

"No, really, what's wrong with you?"

He pinched the ticklish spot in her side and she squealed and squirmed. "Maybe I've changed. Or maybe I owe you."

"That's true—I've held your hand through about four dozen breakups with differing versions of Barbie."

"Yeah because I was really sad when I broke up with whatever their names were," he said. "You know me—I cling."

"Lucky for you there is always another woman around the corner, waiting to soothe your broken heart," Melly said.

"Hey, I haven't had a girlfriend in…" he paused, doing a mental calculation. "In a long time," he added lamely, not wanting to point out the obvious fact that he hadn't dated anyone since Lolly died. He really must be mental to have remained dateless for so long. "What about you? You barely date anyone in three years and then you settle for *Robert?*"

"What's wrong with Robert? He's a doctor, a children's doctor. He's brilliant and kindhearted."

"What? Sorry. I fell asleep as soon as I said his name."

"He is not boring," Melly said, growing defensive.

"Name one interesting thing about him."

"Doctor."

"That's another word for science nerd. Name something else."

"He hikes."

"I scale mountains and jump out of airplanes. Next."

"It's not a competition between you and Robert," Melly said.

"Why not? You should compare every may you date to me," he said.

"I do, and if they remind me of you, I don't date them," Melly said.

"Melly," he said, his tone affronted.

"Do we need to revisit the forty eight girlfriends you've had since I've known you? Or your huge, giant head that can barely fit in the same room with your body?"

"Those are merely personality quirks," Kelsey said. "Everyone has them. What about all the reasons you should compare other men to me and find them lacking?"

"Name one," she said.

In answer, he tipped her face up and kissed her. And kissed her, and kissed her because there was no such thing as a short kiss with Melly, apparently. At last she put her hands on his chest and pushed, wrenching herself away from the gentle pressure of his mouth. They were both suddenly hyper aware of the fact that she was in his arms, in a hotel room. Alone.

"We should tell someone you found me, don't you think?" Melly asked. She licked her chafed lips, sounding nervous.

Kelsey nodded, dazed. What happened here? Had he actually kissed her? He hadn't meant to. She scurried out of his embrace and backed away while he pulled out his phone and called Nick.

"I found Melly."

"What's wrong? Is she okay?" Nick sounded panicked, and Kelsey realized his voice had sounded as odd and strained as he felt. He cleared his throat and tried again.

"She's fine. She had no idea we would be looking for her or worried about her, she needed to clear her head." His eyes narrowed on Melly as she paced beside the bed. They still hadn't gotten to the reason she made her escape. "I'll bring her home soon and we'll talk to you later."

"Sounds good." Nick paused. "How are you holding up?"

"The crazy is being held at bay for the moment," Kelsey replied, chagrined Nick would feel the need to check up on him when Melly was the one with the problem.

"Okay, point taken; I'll stop mother henning you," Nick said. "I wanted you to know we're here if you or Melly need anything."

"I already knew," Kelsey said. "Shouldn't you be in church by now?" Nick was a regular church attender since meeting his wife, something else Kelsey found hilarious.

"I'm there now and Ashleigh is giving me the eye. Later."

Kelsey tucked his phone in his pocket. "Mel, we need to talk."

She shook her head and closed her eyes, the nonverbal equivalent of "La, la, la, I can't hear you."

"I need to know why you're here."

She stopped short and looked at him. "Oh, that."

Did she really think he was going to make her talk about the kiss he was also trying to pretend never happened? "Yes, that."

She sank onto the bed and fished in her pocket. "I got this," she said. She held the note out for his inspection. He took it from her and read it out loud.

"I know about your daughter. Tell anyone what happened, and I'll kill her."

"The postmark was from California," she said.

"How old is your daughter?" Kelsey asked; the words felt odd on his tongue. He still couldn't believe of all the people in the world, Mellisandra Garcia had an illegitimate, secret daughter with a married man.

"She's nine."

"Why do you think you got this now?" he asked.

Melly took a breath. "Her father, her biological father, is running for the senate."

"State senate?" Kelsey asked.

"No, *the* senate. Someone must have found out about her and they're afraid I'm going to come forward with information. Of course I'm not, but what if they believe I am? What if they hurt her anyway? What am I going to do, Kelsey?"

"We'll figure it out," Kelsey said. He had to swallow down a lump of rage to get the words out. Someone had threatened Melly's daughter, thereby hurting and scaring Melly, and there would be retribution.

"I don't want you getting involved," Melly said.

"Why not?"

"Because you've got that look, the same one Jesus used to get, like you're out for blood."

"That's because I am," Kelsey said.

"You're not risking your career or prison over this, over me."

"Why don't you let me worry about what I will or won't risk over you?" He looked down at the note still in his hand. "Can you take some time off work?"

"Yes. I haven't used my personal days, and I've never taken a sick day. Why?"

"Because we're going to come at this thing head on. We're going to go to California and figure out who sent this."

"I guess at the very least I'm going to have to find my daughter's parents and warn them," Melly said.

"That's good, but that's not all we're doing. We're going to flush them out and resolve the situation."

"I don't like that idea," Melly said. "This isn't a game; this is my daughter's life on the line."

"And you want to keep taking chances with it? What if the guy gets elected and someone decides it's too much risk that he'll get unelected? Or what if this comes up every time he's up for reelection? Or what if he runs for president? You don't skulk around waiting for an enemy to strike, Melly. You draw them out and take them down."

She bit her lip, staring at him as she considered. He felt like the weight of her faith in him hung in the balance, and he was disconcerted by how much he wanted her to trust him.

"I won't let anything happen to you or your daughter," Kelsey promised.

"I don't care what happens to me, I only care that she's safe," Melly said.

Kelsey didn't like the physical distance between them when a few moments ago they had been so close. He left the shabby chair and sat next to her on the bed. "I care what happens to you," he said. He gave her a light shove. She fell back against the bed, looking up at him with wide eyes that threatened to flee if he kissed her again. He had no intention of walking into that minefield, but he did need to hold her. He gathered her close and spoke softly. "I missed you these last few months. I'm sorry I was a jerk, sorry I left you alone, sorry about the way I behaved at the wedding. I realize you don't have to forgive me, but I hope you will. I miss my best friend. *Yo quiero mi* Melly," he added to make her laugh, but she didn't laugh. She started to cry again. And, in a way, it was like a gift. She had never given in to her emotions this way in front of him before, never opened up and allowed him to comfort her.

Now she burrowed her face against his neck and clung. He pressed her close, trying to absorb her warmth and Mellyness. How had he gone so long without her when she was vital to his wellbeing? He used the opportunity to run his hands over her, enjoying her warmth and softness. No one was as soft as Melly, and he couldn't quite figure out why that was. She wasn't overweight. Her figure was pleasantly rounded. When he was with other women, though, they didn't feel the same. If women were coats, then others were cotton or polyester and Melly was the real deal—she was all mink.

"Why are you petting me like a cat?" she asked as her tears began to dissolve.

"Trust me when I say you don't want to know," Kelsey said. She would not appreciate the mink comparison, but it was apt. She was sleek, silky, soft, wily, and occasionally mean enough to bite the head off a chicken. He smiled and she pulled back, eyes narrowing.

"I don't understand you at all today," she said.

"I'm growing as a human being," he said.

"Stop. You're freaking me out. Go back to being arrogant and shallow and let's not upset the status quo." She framed his face with her hands and inspected his features.

He smiled because he knew she was appreciating his beauty. She did it a lot, like one might appreciate a painting in a museum with no intention of buying. "Nope. I'm deep now—I'm the total package."

Melly didn't reply. Instead her thumb moved lower and began tracing his bottom lip. A familiar light began to flicker in her eyes, one he liked to call the moth-to-a-flame look because women often got it when they were near him. They were drawn to his good looks and sparkling personality—they couldn't help themselves. Except Melly had never had that look before with him, and now he was the one who was freaking out. He couldn't go there, *they* couldn't go there, not when things were getting back on track.

"What are you doing?" he asked, giving her a little shake so she bounced up and down on the bed. She came to like someone waking from sleep.

"What?" She sprang away and drew back her hand. "I don't know. Why do you have to be so stinking pretty? Geez, you're like catnip for humans." She shoved away from him and stood up, stumbling a little until she righted herself.

"Yeah? Tell me more," he said, propping his arm behind his head. Surly Melly and Cocky Kelsey was their usual M/O, but Kelsey's cockiness was forced. He felt off-kilter with the thought that Melly might actually be attracted to him. His heart was beating so hard he was surprised she couldn't hear it from where she stood.

"Maybe later," she said, turning her back to him as she smoothed her hand over her hair. She was aiming for surly, but her hand shook, ruining the effect. "We should go."

He stood. He wanted things to go back to the way they had been before, with no weirdness between them. Then he had been able to joke with her, to be affectionate with her, with no awkward tension hovering between them. Now something was different, and he didn't like it. "Melly," he began.

She turned toward him and let down her hair, running her fingers through the mass so it tumbled down and cascaded onto her shoulders. "What?"

His mouth went dry. Had he ever seen her do that before? Her hair was so thick and lush; it must weigh a ton. He scrapped whatever he had intended to say, which was a good plan since he could no longer remember what it was. "Do you ever get headaches from your hair?" he asked instead.

She blinked at him, trying to figure the direction of his thoughts. "Sometimes. I have one now, but I haven't eaten in a while."

Now was the time to say something clever and quippy and get out of here. "Oh," he said instead as he took a step forward and plunged his fingers in her hair, massaging her scalp. Her hair was over the top, as was her beauty. If she applied herself and learned how to work it, she could have men eating out of her hand. She could probably go to Hollywood and be famous. But she did none of those things. She didn't even seem to notice or understand how pretty she was, which made her all the more intriguing. She was a study in contrasts, something that normally frustrated Kelsey. He didn't do complex. He liked his women straightforward and simple. Stupid, really. The dumb bimbo thing worked for him. But Melly was beginning to intrigue him in a way she never had before. What made her tick? How was such a luscious beauty also a type-A book nerd? She taught kindergarten when by all rights she should be on a pin-up calendar somewhere. She looked innocent and untouched, but she was someone's mother.

The hair thing was definitely working. At the first touch of his fingers, she melted, leaning against him while her fingers dug his chest for support. This was another first, and another contrast. Melly usually looked so prim and frosty, as if one's fingers might freeze and snap off if he actually dared to touch her. But touch her and she went up in flames. She was killing him, and not in a good way. He didn't like all this mental chatter filling up his brain. She should come with a manual.

"Your hair is properly tousled now," he said. His throat sounded croaky, as if he had spent a lot of time screaming. He forced himself to withdraw his fingers from her hair and take a step back, putting out a hand to catch her when she nearly fell over.

She came to again as if rousing from a dream, clearing her throat with a deep blush. "I like to have my hair played with. I guess we've never discussed that before."

"Duly noted." With a plan to never, ever repeat. What was the heat set on in this room? It was like a hundred and ten degrees. Kelsey tugged his collar. "We should go. I need to arrange our flights."

"I can do that," Melly said, trying hard to be all business again.

Kelsey shook his head. "If I do it, then I can use my military discount."

"At least let me pay for it," she insisted.

Before he would have smiled and said of course she was paying, but he couldn't bring himself to do it. He owed her so much more than a couple of plane tickets. "This one's on me. You can pay the next time we jet off to some far-flung locale."

She laughed, but the sound came out more nervous than amused. "I need to pack."

"Let's go then." He held the door for her, and she walked out, being extra careful not to touch him again.

CHAPTER 7

There was silence in the car, and not the good kind. Silence could occasionally be thoughtful or intimate. This silence was awkward and oppressive. Kelsey was usually good at filling empty spaces with mindless chatter, but he was drawing a blank, and Melly wasn't helping. She stared out the window, her finger nervously twining her hair. As soon as they parked in her driveway, she jetted out of the vehicle like her tail was on fire.

The first person they encountered inside the house was Shelby. Melly hugged her fiercely. "I'm so sorry, Shelby. I wasn't thinking clearly. I didn't mean to make you worry."

"It's okay," Shelby said, returning the hug with equal ferocity while Truck and Kelsey hovered in the background. Then Truck stepped forward and rested his hand on Melly's shoulder.

"Everything okay, Mel?" he asked.

Kelsey shifted impatiently. His jealousy was unwarranted because it wasn't like that between them, but Melly was his responsibility, *his*. Truck had enough on his plate with Shelby, although she seemed much better than he would have expected. If one didn't know about the trauma she had suffered, then there would be no way to tell by looking. Kelsey knew, however, that she had undergone months of therapy, as had Truck.

"I'm okay," Melly said.

Truck nodded and dropped his hand. "We were going out for brunch. Want to grab something with us?"

"Thanks, but I have some things to do," Melly said. "You guys have a good time. And, again, I'm really sorry about all the worry. I wasn't thinking."

"Forget about it," Truck said. He eased his arm around Shelby and squeezed Melly's bicep with his free hand.

He's certainly multi-tasking the women in the room, Kelsey thought. Truck gave him an odd look as he passed, as if he sensed his jealous thoughts, and then Shelby and Truck were gone, leaving Melly and Kelsey alone in the silent house.

"What's that look for?" Melly asked, hands on hips as she whirled to face him.

Apparently his poker face stunk. He drew breath to blast her with his jealousy and then reconsidered. She was dealing with enough right now, and it was irrational anyway. Truck wasn't interested in Melly, and Melly wasn't interested in Truck. They were friends. Everyone in their group was close, and that was how Kelsey wanted it, like family. "Nothing, my own stupidity," he said at last.

Melly's expression turned inexplicably wounded. "Kelsey," she intoned, thumping her foot on the floor in a display of frustration.

"What?" he asked, totally clueless. Melly had always loathed what she called his immature displays of jealousy and possessiveness. Wouldn't it stand to reason his new maturity would make her happy?

Nick and Ashleigh came home then, saving them from a discussion. Melly hugged Nick with a muttered apology and then latched on to Ashleigh like a lifeline. "I need your help," she said, dragging Ashleigh behind as she led her to her bedroom. Ashleigh threw a questioning look at Kelsey over her shoulder, but he shrugged. He had no idea what was eating Melly. She had apparently gone off the deep end.

* * *

"I'M LOSING IT, ASHLEIGH," Melly said as soon as they were safely inside her room. She threw herself across the bed, not caring that she might mess up her bed. Then she realized Kelsey had slept there. Not only did he leave it unmade, but it smelled like him. She groaned and rolled away, but his scent followed her.

"You scared us," Ashleigh said, her tone wary as if she wasn't quite sure how to proceed. She was a down-to-earth person, but Melly was so stolid that Ashleigh seemed flighty in comparison. And now the usually rock-steady Melly was losing it at an alarming rate.

"Sorry," Melly said. "That was a colossal misunderstanding. I was simply trying to get away to think. I had no idea anyone would miss me. I forgot I have a roommate now. But I was actually talking about Kelsey."

"What about him?"

"He kissed me."

Ashleigh waited for more, but nothing came. "So? You guys have kissed before."

"Twice, and both times I was in control. And both times it was to make him shut up. This was different. This was real." *And I wasn't in control at all,* she thought, remembering the way she had reacted to Kelsey, to the kiss. She had melted like any mindless teenager who gets kissed by a beautiful man. "He's not acting like Kelsey."

"What do you mean?"

"He's being sweet, and not the usual I-want-something-so-I'm-going-to-be-nice-to-you ploy. I mean genuinely sweet."

Ashleigh walked over to her and rested her hands on her shoulders. "You made me swear that if you ever began to act like one of Kelsey's groupies that I would shake you and tell you to snap out of it. This is me shaking you and telling you to snap out of it. I love the man, but I don't want to see you get hurt, Melly. Kelsey loves women, and then he leaves them. That's his thing. Don't be fooled by the charm."

"I know. I agree with everything you said. What is wrong with me?

I counsel women like me from falling for guys like him. I could write a book on all the ways being with Kelsey is a bad idea, and I could write a book on all the ways to avoid the pitfall. And here I am, rushing headlong into attraction for him like a dope."

She plopped back onto the bed and threw her arms over her face.

"Your defenses are low," Ashleigh said. "It's been a rough time lately, and you're not desensitized to him like normal because you guys have spent so much time apart. You need to take a step back, take a breather, and pull yourself together."

"That would be great if we weren't flying to California today."

"What?" Ashleigh exploded before lowering her voice to a furious whisper. "You cannot go to California with him, Melly. That's where he's from—he'll have home court advantage. He's probably even more charming there."

"It's also where I'm from, Ash, and I've got to go back."

"Why? What's wrong?" Ashleigh nudged her aside and lay down beside her, resting her chin on her arms.

Melly got up, retrieved her box from the closet and came back. She rifled through the box until she located the pictures and then she handed them over. "This is my daughter," she said. She wasn't trying to be dramatic, but her pronouncement had that effect because Ashleigh's jaw dropped as she stared at the pictures, speechless. "Someone is threatening her. Kelsey thinks the best course of action is to go and flush them out."

Ashleigh set the pictures aside and put her arms around Melly. "You've had a lot on your plate."

Melly returned her clasp, resting her head on Ashleigh's shoulder. She hadn't realized how much she had been longing for Ashleigh's acceptance until she had it. Ashleigh was the type of person Melly used to be, wholly innocent and intact. Even though she knew in her head Ashleigh wouldn't reject her once she found out about her glaring failure, her ready acceptance was still a blessed relief.

"What can Nick and I do?" Ashleigh continued. "Do you want us to come with you? I'm not certain Nick could get away, but I could."

Melly was tempted. Ashleigh and Kelsey often butted heads,

albeit gently. She would be the perfect chaperone to save Melly from herself. But it wasn't fair to drag someone away when she already rarely got to see her husband because of his job. And Melly was a grownup; she had never relied on anyone to do things for her that she should be capable of doing herself. She knew better than to fall for Kelsey—she simply had to start listening to her own good sense.

"No, thanks. I'll be okay. It's only Kelsey, right? How hard could it be to avoid falling for him? I've done it successfully and consistently for three years. No need to change that now." She said it as much to herself as to Ashleigh.

There was a tap on the door and Kelsey and Nick poked their heads inside. "Hey, I scheduled our flights. Nick and Ashleigh are going to drive us to the airport. We leave in an hour. Is there anything I can do to help? I'm sort of a pro at packing on short notice, you know," Kelsey said. He smiled and it was devoid of his usual smug arrogance.

"No, I'm good. Ashleigh's helping," Melly said.

"Yes, I see that," Kelsey said, taking note of their prone positions across the bed. "Snap to it, Luscious. We're wheels up by fourteen hundred." He backed out of the room, taking Nick with him.

"What was that?" Ashleigh whispered.

"I know, right? It's like invasion of the body snatchers. Suddenly Kelsey is responsible and compassionate."

Ashleigh blew out a breath and shook her head. "You are in serious trouble, sister."

Melly thumped her fist against her forehead. "I need to think of all the careless, cruddy stuff he's done to me over the years. Like the time he couldn't find his credit card and used mine to buy his girlfriend a tooth-whitening treatment."

"That time when you and Lolly went on vacation and he forgot to check on your house and the basement flooded," Ashleigh added.

"That time he signed me up for premium cable because he wanted to watch a game and didn't think I would notice the extra package on my bill, and then I couldn't get rid of it for a year," Melly said.

"The crazy cult at the airport he gave your number to," Ashleigh said.

Melly sputtered a laugh. "That one was kind of funny. Plus I got him back by signing him up for that dating site where everyone has their picture taken with their pet."

"That was a good one," Ashleigh said. She held out her fist, and Melly bumped it.

"Yeah, but then he ended up dating five women from that site," Melly said, chagrined. "Made me feel like the person who introduced rabbits to Australia."

Ashleigh snickered. They lay in silence a few beats. "Your daughter is beautiful. What's her name?"

"I named her Anna. Her adoptive parents named her something else. I don't know what. They send me a picture a year, as per our original agreement, but I don't know anything about her." *Except her address.* She knew that because of a careless mistake. She had never used it before, but all that was about to change. There was a chance that she might actually get to see her little girl in person, and she wasn't at all ready.

Ashleigh reached out and took her hand, giving it a squeeze. "I'm here for you. If you need anything, if you want to talk, to vent, to cry, to laugh—I'm here. Anytime."

"I know. Thanks." She smiled.

"And don't kiss Kelsey again." She let go her hand and wound their pinkies together. "Swear it."

"I swear," Melly said, and she meant it. "I won't kiss him again."

"Or let him kiss you," Ashleigh added.

"Or let him kiss me. Promise."

Ashleigh nodded. "It's official. You pinky swore. Dire things will happen if you break the vow."

"Like what?" Melly asked.

"Like you'll get your heart broken," Ashleigh said.

Melly groaned. "If I somehow end up as one of Kelsey Adams's hapless victims, I can never hold my head up again."

"Then don't. You're Melly Garcia. You're a fool for no man."

"That's not exactly true," Melly said. "I was a fool once, a terrible fool. That's how I learned not to be one again."

"Then remember. You've been through too much to be hurt again, Melly. Man up, so to speak."

Melly took a bracing breath and rolled off the bed. "You're right, of course. Step one is to stop talking about it like we're in eighth grade again. Help me pick out some clothes because I'm not really thinking clearly right now." With effort they turned their focus to packing, not mentioning Kelsey again until they parted ways at the airport.

CHAPTER 8

Melly was giving him the silent treatment again. Kelsey scanned his memory for whatever might have set her off, but he could think of nothing. Maybe she was simply nervous. He reached over the seat to take her hand, but she ripped it away.

"Melly, what the crud?" he said. "Why are you so mad at me?"

She looked at him in confusion. "Mad at you? I'm not mad at you."

"Then why won't you talk to me or touch me?" he asked. "You never actually said if you forgave me." His too-handsome face crumpled into a pout, and Melly's anxiety eased. A pouting, immature, whiny Kelsey she could deal with.

"Of course I forgive you, Kelsey. I'm sorry if I'm acting crazy."

"Not if. You are."

"Okay, I'll concede I'm a little off my game. I'm overwhelmed, and I'm taking it out on you. I'm sorry." She reached for his hand this time. She would have clasped it, but he wove their fingers together.

"What were you and Ashleigh talking about in your room? Was it me? I bet it was me."

"Contrary to popular belief, the world does not revolve around you," she hedged. "I told her about Anna."

"Is that her name? Your little girl?"

87

She swallowed down an unbidden lump. *My little girl.* "That was her name, but she's not really mine anymore. She was only mine for three hours." Still, she remembered every detail, every smell. Even her cry still echoed in her head.

"I was only four when my mom died, but she's still my mom. Most of my childhood memories are of my grandmother, but there's a special bond for the woman who gave you life. Someday you'll have more kids, and maybe it won't hurt so much. I bet Dr. Bob wants loads of kids, huh?"

Melly sat up in alarm. "Oh, no, Robert. I forgot to call him." She put her hand to her head. "What is wrong with me? How could I forget to make contact, forget to tell him I'm going out of town?"

"Because you're just not that into him?" Kelsey suggested.

"No, that's not true. I like him a lot."

"Do you lurve him? I saw that he said the L-word on his cards. Have you said it back?"

"In what galaxy would I possibly share that information with you?" Melly asked.

"In the one where we're friends and I'm entitled to know the pertinent details of your life," Kelsey replied.

"I am not discussing another man with you."

"Why not? I talk about other women with you."

"Despite my repeated protests," she interjected.

He ignored her. "Maybe it's because you know Dr. Bob doesn't measure up. Talking about him with me makes you realize that he comes up, uh, short."

"Stop making fun of him."

He gave her a falsely innocent look. "Did I say a word about his height? Now that you bring it up, though, have you been able to get him to tell you where he keeps his pot of gold?"

"Kelsey, enough. Robert is the nicest guy I have ever dated. He's hard working, devoted, and he treats me like a queen. What possible objection could you have against him?"

He's not me. The thought came out of nowhere, stunning him. He was possessive of Melly the way he was possessive of anyone who wasn't doting on him. But he had never realized before that he was actually jealous of Melly's boyfriend. *Time to employ a little honesty.* "You're so beautiful, Melly. Do you even realize how beautiful you are? You could have anyone. I hate to think of you settling for the first nice guy who comes along."

"Kelsey," she said, her tone exasperated as tears sprang to her eyes again. She turned to the window and shook free of his hand so she could wipe them away.

"What? I'm being honest. Isn't that what you've been saying you want me to be for years? Real? This is me being real, and now you don't like it."

"I like it, okay?" she said. *I like it too much; you're killing me.* "Haven't you ever heard that old saying 'Be careful what you wish for because you might get it?'"

"No, and it's weird. Why wouldn't you want whatever you wished for? You're like the most complex person on the planet, Melly. Would it be so wrong for you to for once, say what you mean and feel instead of keeping everything bottled inside all the time?"

Yes. It would be devastating for her to give in to her carefully constructed walls, especially now, especially with Kelsey. They had always maintained a sort of parent-child relationship with Melly being the mother figure and Kelsey being the errant child. Only now he was sounding and acting like a grown man and Melly was genuinely frightened of the implications. She took a breath.

"I'm trying to survive this ordeal intact, okay?" she said.

"Okay," he said, reaching for her hand again. They sat in silence a few seconds, but silence never lasted long with Kelsey. Today was no exception. "I was thinking maybe we should get a dog."

"We?" Melly said quirking an eyebrow.

"My, uh, therapist said it might help with my PTSD. But I'm gone so much that he would have to live with you part time."

Melly bit her lip, thinking. The thought of having a pet, even part time, was suddenly appealing. "Can we get one that doesn't shed?"

"Like one of those weird hairless ones?" Kelsey asked, lip curled. "I was thinking something big and manly."

"No, not a hairless dog. But they have varieties that don't shed much like poodle mixes or wiry terriers." She sat up now, feeling excited over the prospect. "Maybe we could look for one when we get back."

"Sounds good," Kelsey said. He gave her hand a squeeze. "A dog together. That's a big step." He wagged his eyebrows. "Maybe now is the time to make a baby pact."

"What are you talking about?" Melly asked.

"You know like if we're forty an unattached we have a baby together."

"I think one experience with being an unwed mother is enough for a lifetime," Melly said, her tone cooling considerably.

"C'mon, Melly, don't be so old-fashioned. I get it; you were a baby then yourself. But you're a grownup now, and you'll be even more mature at forty. What's the big deal? It's not like being an unwed mother has the same stigma it used to."

"It does to me," she said.

"That's an outdated way of thinking. No one cares anymore. It's no big deal." Melly rested her head against the seat and smiled at him. "What?"

"Keep talking—it's working."

"What's working?"

"Nothing. I'm appreciating the vast differences between us," Melly replied. She breathed a sigh of relief. The morning's aberration had been corrected; Kelsey was Kelsey and always would be. There was no way she could consider being with someone who didn't share her most fundamental beliefs.

Kelsey, on the other hand, seemed irritated by her placid smile. "You're doing it again," he accused.

"What?"

"Disappearing behind your Melly shield. I can see you doing it. Don't you think I know when you're blocking me?" He crossed his arms over his chest and slouched, scowling. Melly grew even happier over his behavior.

"Kelsey, you are one of my best friends in the world, and I love you. Nothing is going to change that."

If possible, his scowl turned even darker. "Don't."

"Don't what?"

"Don't condescend, Melly. You are not my mother. We're the same age."

"I'm not trying to condescend, Kelsey. You are a very capable man and marine. But you and I are different."

"We're not," Kelsey argued.

"We are."

"We aren't. I grew up like you, with all the religious stuff—church on Sunday, prayer before meals, crud like that. The only difference between us is that I grew out of it and you've held on. And I'm not saying there's anything wrong with that. To each his own. Why can't you believe what you want and I *not* believe what I want? Why does it have to be your way or nothing?"

"Because it does. Because anything less for me is a compromise. Sure, in theory it sounds good to say if we're not attached at forty then we'll have a baby together, but the practical implications are a minefield," she said.

"Like what?"

"Like whose name would he take?"

"Mine," he blurted.

"Why? We're not married. Why would he have to take your name? Why can't he be a Garcia? Who would he live with? What would he tell his friends about why we're not married? Who would pay for stuff like clothes, sports, and braces? What happens when I want him to take piano lessons and you want him to play football?"

He rolled his eyes. "Geez, Melly, it's hypothetical. Way to suck the fun from the game."

"I know it's hypothetical, Kelsey. I'm merely trying to answer your question as to why the differences between us matter. We believe different things; we want different things. You can do casual and no strings; I can't. I want marriage, commitment, and a family, and I won't settle for anything less."

"And you think little Dr. Bob is going to be the one to give you those things?" His curled lip let her know what he thought of that idea. "Your child would need a step ladder to reach a toadstool."

Melly couldn't help but give an exasperated chuckle at his revulsion. "Maybe, but I'm in no rush. Like you've pointed out at least a million times, we're only twenty seven. There's no rush."

"I'm glad you listen to at least something I say."

"Every once in a while you make a good point," Melly said. "It usually coincides with the leap year."

"Watch it, Garcia. This head is chock full of useful wisdom, even more so now that it's been shrunk."

"I can't believe you're actually going to therapy."

"You gave me an ultimatum," he said. "See what a good friend I am?"

She quirked an eyebrow and he resisted the urge to squirm. How did she *do* that? How did she so easily see through his lies to the truth?

"Fine. Nick gave me an ultimatum, and I found that I value my career more than my pride."

"How is it?"

One shoulder flopped up and down in a shrug. "Not as bad as I thought. Marilyn—that's her name—is pretty cool. At least she makes me laugh."

"High praise," Melly said.

He smiled because she knew him so well.

"Is it helping?" she asked, her tone tentative once again.

"I guess so. I didn't realize I was so messed up." He paused, clearing his throat. "I, uh, gave up drinking, at least for a while. What happened with you at the wedding, it scared me." He stared at the *SkyMall* catalogue in front of him as if he found its products irresistible. Melly rested her hand on his leg and gave it a pat.

"I'm glad things are getting better, Kelse. You had me worried."

He picked up her hand in both his, bringing it to his lips to bestow something between a nibble and a kiss. "You worried about me, Mel?"

"Since the day I met you," she said. Her flippant tone fell flat as the air between them crackled with the strange chemistry once again.

One of his hands let go of hers and lightly touched the hair at her temple.

"Why, Melly? Why do you care? Why do you waste your time on me if you think I'm so hopeless?"

She opened her mouth to answer, but the words stuck. The truth was that she didn't think he was hopeless. She wanted to—she wanted to pretend he was the shallow, egotistical jerk she accused him of being. But there were times, like now, when she saw glimmers of greatness in him, the same greatness Jesus had seen. Kelsey could be a good man; he could be the best man she knew if he got his act together. For the past three years, that had been her desperate wish, that Kelsey would grow up and stop acting like an adolescent playboy. But now that she was on the cusp of receiving her wish, she was suddenly terrified. If Kelsey turned into the man she had always dreamed of, what did that mean for her? What excuse could she offer to keep herself away from him? And, looking as he did, if he suddenly grew into a man she could love, how could she resist?

"I guess it's the teacher in me," she lied. "We never stop hoping we'll be able to touch that unreachable student."

Far from being offended, Kelsey gave her a smile as if he could read her inmost soul, as if he knew the truth. "I'm right here. Touch me if you want, Miss Garcia." He kissed her hand again and it was such a typically Kelsey line that Melly laughed and plucked her hand from his grasp, shoving his arm when she was free.

"You probably were that kid who charmed your teachers and got away with murder," Melly said.

"Maybe if I ever had a teacher who looked like you, I might have tried hard to make that true. As it was, teachers didn't like me. Too talkative and squirmy. It's really unfair to make hyper little boys sit in a chair for eight hours." He became irritated, remembering how difficult it had been to sit still all those many years ago. He had lived for recess and gym class.

"That's old school," Melly said. "Today we have to adapt to all learning styles. There's not too much sitting still in my classroom, though there is a time and place for quiet learning."

He let go her hand and wrapped his arms around her, nuzzling his nose against her face as he kissed her cheek. "You're a great teacher, Melly."

She smiled and returned the impromptu embrace. "How do you know?"

"I just do."

She closed her eyes and savored the embrace, resting her head on his shoulder. When they first met, his spontaneous displays of affection had irritated her because she had thought he was hitting on her. Unlike him, she wasn't free with her feelings or her affection. Over time, she had come to understand this was who he was. He wasn't like this with the women he dated, free and loving. With them, he was always "on," always the charming ladies' man, quick with a flirtatious comment or innuendo. It was only with her that he unbent enough to give her a hug for no reason or pick her up and twirl her around because he was having a good day. She would never admit it, but she loved every touch because it was honest and because she needed it. With Jesus gone, Kelsey was the only person left to hug and be hugged in return.

Thoughts of her brother rose up and crashed against her already fragmented emotions. The hug quickly turned from lighthearted to desperate as Melly clung to him, pressing her face to his neck. His touch seemed to be the only buffer between her and a tidal wave of despair.

"I missed you," she admitted, the words wrenching free with effort. Melly hated being vulnerable, hated admitting she had needs. Admitting how much she had missed his friendship was tantamount to handing him the emotional reins of their relationship, something she had never done. In the past, she had always maintained the upper hand. What would he do with so much control? She swallowed hard, waiting to find out.

He paused, a little stunned by her admission. Melly was acting very un-Melly, and it was throwing him off his game. His first impulse was to make a joke, to ask her to prove how much she had missed him with a kiss. But Lolly's face and Lolly's promise held him back. *Take care of Melly for me; swear it.* "I'm here, Melly, and I'm not going anywhere again. Deal?"

She nodded, but she didn't speak or look up. The plane started to descend. Kelsey let her go and eased away, clumsily swiping at her tears with his fingers. He had never been good with tears; he was better with laughter, or even anger. The sight of Melly's tears was especially painful, though not as scary as he had first imagined. He felt no temptation to flee, only to make her feel better. He was unconsciously cupping her face with his free hand while he swiped at her tears. Melly watched him, her ebony eyes luminous and filled with an unbearable tenderness. Now it was Kelsey's turn to freeze, his breath catching in surprise. This person truly cared about him, much more than most people he knew, much more than she rightfully should. He had repeatedly trod on her, trampling her personal space, purposely irritating her to get a reaction, and then ignoring her when she needed him most. Yet he read no censure in her expression, only a deep affinity, boundless loyalty and friendship.

She made him wonder if perhaps there was a God after all because, as certain as he was breathing, he knew he had never done anything good enough to deserve someone like her in his life. She had been a gift, and Lolly, too. They had graced his life with a steadfast sort of unconditional love he was only beginning to appreciate.

And suddenly it was there again, that overwhelming desire to kiss her, to put his mark on her, to lay claim to a bit of her perfection. He was bewildered by the new uncomfortable thoughts and so he let her go, dropping his hand as he backed away and groped his mind for a joke to relieve the pressure of the moment.

"Do you think anyone ever pulls down one of those oxygen masks and takes a hit for the fun of it?" he asked, though he wasn't quite kidding. He could use the extra boost of O2 right about now.

This was the point where Melly was supposed to respond with a wry, witty comeback, but she didn't. "I don't know," she said instead, sitting back to stare dazedly out the window. Together, they finished the flight in silence.

CHAPTER 9

The silence continued as Melly and Kelsey disembarked the plane. For once, Melly was the one who couldn't take the disconcerting stillness any longer. She had to say something, anything.

"Where did you book us?" she asked as they headed to their rental car. She hadn't considered their transportation—Kelsey had apparently thought of everything.

"I didn't," he said. His tone alerted her to the fact that she wasn't going to like what he was about to impart. "We're staying with an old friend of mine."

Melly sighed. "What's her name?"

"Joan."

"Joan? You dated a Joan?" The name Joan conjured a studious woman who spent her time at the library or finishing needlework, certainly not Kelsey's usual type.

"It was a long time ago," he explained.

"Kelsey!" A woman's voice shrieked his name loudly enough to shatter the thick glass airport windows. Melly and Kelsey stopped as the woman ran at them, at him, really, and propelled herself into his arms.

"Oh, *Joan*," Melly said because now the name made more sense. She was probably 5'8" with long blond hair and big blue eyes, and a perfect figure, if one thought being top-heavy made for a perfect figure, which Kelsey did. Melly was tempted to ask her if she did needlework to see the baffled look on her face.

Kelsey eased away from Joan with the look he always had when confronted with an ex-girlfriend. It was an expression that said he felt so trapped he would willingly gnaw his own leg to get away. Melly was used to it because he often wore that look. Seemingly they couldn't go anywhere without running into someone he had dumped, not even a couple of thousand miles away in California. She was also used to what came next because Kelsey did it whenever he wanted an easy out with one of the women. He slipped his arm around Melly's shoulders and gave them a squeeze.

"Joanie, this is Melly," he said. He didn't actually lie and say the words, "She's my girlfriend," but his tone and touch conveyed the thought as clearly as if he had spoken. Melly's usual response was to either jab him in the ribs, walk away and wish him luck, or turn on her own cling factor to scare the pants off him. But today she owed him, the jerk.

"It's so nice to meet one of Kelsey's friends," she said, politely extending her hand to Joan. "I've heard a little about you." *Your name, for instance.* Joan beamed at this news, though her thousand-watt smile was directed at Kelsey.

"I guess he told you we were high school sweethearts. We dated for almost two years, and then he joined up and broke my heart." She jutted one of her perfectly sculpted lips as her eyes turned wide, wounded, and yearning for what might have been.

Melly resisted the urge to choke. Kelsey definitely hadn't mentioned he and *Joanie* were high school sweethearts, or that he had a high school sweetheart, or that he had ever dated anyone longer than three weeks. Two years?! Melly had never been jealous of any of Kelsey's women until now. Two years was not a fling; two years was a legitimate and committed relationship, even if they had been kids. She resisted the urge to tell Joan the truth, however, feeling it would give the other woman an advantage. Instead she bestowed a sultry smile on Kelsey.

"Kelsey's suddenly full of mystery, aren't you, Babe?" Her hand rested gently on his chest and gave it a pat and her eyes—which were usually filled with murderous indignation by this point in the game—were hooded with something that looked like a combination of flirtation and jealousy. Jealousy? Could that be right?

Kelsey blinked down at her in surprise. Usually in these situations she sought retribution, either by making up an outrageous fact—such as the time she had told a girlfriend that he rode a horse bareback and serenaded her with a synthesizer outside her room—or she made up a sickening nickname, like *schmoopems,* to let him know she was irritated. Never had she rallied to the occasion and acted the part. He wasn't quite sure what to do next.

"I would say you know more than your fair share of my secrets, Mel," he said, offering up a tentative smile.

She winked at him. Melly, who usually only flirted with him after a whole lot of arguing first, looked up at him with her beautiful black eyes and billions of long lashes and winked. What was up with the world? Suddenly black was white, up was down, and Melly was…he didn't know what Melly was, but she wasn't her normal self. Joan shifted, alerting him to the fact that he had temporarily forgotten her. In his defense, though, he had temporarily forgotten everyone. It was as if the airport noise and chaos faded away, and it was him and Melly staring each other down, trying to figure the other one out. His heart was beating like he had run from enemy fire, and he couldn't understand why. Something monumental was happening, but he was at a loss to put a name to it.

With effort, they tore their gazes apart and focused on Joan who looked none the worse for wear after their little byplay. She was still focused on Kelsey like he held the key to all life's dreams for her. "Ready to go back to my place?" she said, as if she and Kelsey had met up in a bar somewhere and things were about to heat up.

You know I'm coming with you, right? Melly wanted to say. Some of her former irritability was returning. What did Kelsey do to these women to keep them hanging on for so long? High school had been a decade ago, and yet Joan apparently hadn't moved on. Kelsey let go of her to pick up their bags, and she was glad. She suddenly wanted to jab him in the solar plexus for all women everywhere. She was sick to death of immature users, of men who played the game, trampling women to get what they wanted, and of women who let them. Where was the self-respect?

Gone, if Joan was any indication. They reached the parking lot and she handed Melly her keys. "You can drive my car if you want. I'll ride with Kelse."

Melly had no reply; she simply stared at the outstretched hand and proffered keys, speechless.

"Actually, Joanie, I think I'd rather Melly ride with me. She's got a lot going on right now. We'll follow you, if that's okay."

"I suppose," Joan said, clearly crestfallen she wouldn't be able to steal a few minutes alone with Kelsey. She left, dragging her feet like some sort of supermodel version of a sad puppy. Kelsey opened the door of the rental car for Melly and waited to speak until he was safely behind the wheel.

"Not a word," he told Melly.

"I was merely going to ask how many states contain women you've dated," Melly said. "And, for the sake of argument, let's count Puerto Rico as a state."

"Jealousy becomes you, Luscious," Kelsey said, sounding much too full of himself.

"I am not jealous," Melly said, not quite truthfully for once. "But I am surprised you never told me about her. I never pictured you in a long term relationship." She turned toward him, studying his profile. Had he and Joan shared some sort of epic love story, or had she been like all his other women—here today and gone tomorrow?

"You know I don't like to dwell on the past," Kelsey said, his moderate tone and even expression giving nothing away.

"Two years is a long relationship, but I guess maybe it's not the same when you're kids," Melly probed.

Kelsey shrugged one shoulder and didn't take his eyes off the busy San Diego traffic.

She turned toward the window, trying not to let her frustration with him show, frustration that grew exponentially when she saw the corner of his mouth turn up in a satisfied smile. He was loving this, the first jealous display she had ever shown over him. Generally, she couldn't care less who he dated or how long. More often than not all she felt was disgust for his behavior and his partner's obvious lack of self-esteem. Despite being gorgeous and charming, Kelsey didn't have much to offer in a dating relationship. He was shallow and a leech, sucking up whatever energy and emotional resources an unwitting female was willing to bestow. Occasionally his girlfriends did catch on and get fed up with his total self-centeredness. Melly felt like sending them a letter of congratulations after the relationship was over. But Joan had held on for two years. Was she really that dumb and needy, or had Kelsey been different then? Had life and a career in the military shaped him into the love-'em-and-leave-'em person he now was? Had he been caring, attentive, and trustworthy at one point? And, if so, had Joan been the recipient of that version of Kelsey? It was that thought that was fueling Melly's newfound jealousy.

"They say you never get over your first love," Kelsey said, sighing.

Melly turned away, secure in the knowledge he was now trying to fan the flames of her jealousy. It had the opposite effect, however, because she was no longer thinking about him. "I guess I'm about to find out," she said.

Kelsey scowled. "What do you mean? You didn't love this man, the father of your baby."

"I felt like I did."

He shook his head. "You were a scared, grieving kid and he preyed on you. That's not love—that's whatever sick, twisted game he was playing. A man doesn't entice someone who is in his care, someone who he has treated as his daughter, someone who is probably less than half his age, unless he is truly messed up."

"Maybe so," Melly admitted. Kelsey's vehement admonition of her former love was making her rethink things, which was confusing.

How much blame for what happened did she deserve? She had always blamed herself for all of it, but Kelsey had a point; the man had been even older than she was now while she had been a naïve innocent. Shouldn't he have known better? Had their relationship been mutual, or had he purposely targeted and seduced her? And, if so, did that mean she had been a victim? She had felt so much shame over what happened that there hadn't been any room for anger. Kelsey seemed to be feeling enough for both of them, but she still wasn't sure it was warranted.

"There's no maybe, Melly; it just is. He didn't love you, and you didn't love him. The end."

"Kelsey has spoken, amen," Melly said, pressing her hands together in mock reverence.

"I am more than a pretty face, and it's time you started to absorb my wisdom."

"Like the time you told me to invest in that Ponzi scheme?" she said.

"Why do you keep bringing that up? That was forever ago."

"It was last year, and you wanted me to cosign a loan so you could invest ten thousand dollars in shampoo."

"It wasn't shampoo. He sold vitamins, too. Besides, you know I was kidding about that. Mostly. But selling that stuff would have given you something to do with your summers."

"I do have something to do with my summers," Melly protested.

"Melly, c'mon. Volunteering to tutor underprivileged children is never going to make you a millionaire. But selling vitamins guaranteed to increase your bust size? Now that was a winning idea." He rested his hand on her leg and gave it a squeeze, bestowing a smile that said *I know I'm trouble, but you love me anyway.*

Melly laughed and shook her head. He was irrepressible, but he made her laugh. Without him, her life would be dull. Robert sprang to mind and her smile waivered. Robert was nice and well settled, if a little boring. Why couldn't she fall in love with him? She knew he loved her because he had told her so. She hadn't said it back, and he hadn't taken offense. *I know we're not at the same place right now, Melly, and that's okay. I can wait; I'm a very patient man.* He was willing to give her time to come around, but what if she never did? What if she never fell in love with him? Would they go on forever as they were? What was that old adage that it was better for the man to be more in love with a woman than for a woman to be more in love with a man? To some extent, Melly agreed. Women had fragile hearts. Men seemed to have more capacity to protect themselves. It would be awful to love someone and not be loved in return, though, no matter one's sex.

"Poor Joan," she blurted.

"Why poor Joan? I was nice to her," Kelsey said, defensive in case Melly was making her usual commentary on his dating life.

"She's obviously still into you. That must hurt," Melly said. "Ten years is a long time to harbor feelings for someone."

"Yeah, it is," Kelsey said. The wistful, resigned tone was back and she turned her head to frown. Had Kelsey loved Joan? Did he still? She wouldn't give him the satisfaction of asking and they made the rest of the trip to Joan's house in silence.

CHAPTER 10

*J*oan lived in a far-flung suburb of San Diego that, with traffic, took over an hour of travel from the airport. She showed them inside her tiny house and led them to a bedroom, *their* bedroom. Melly looked at Kelsey and he pled with her not to protest. Under normal circumstances, she would have. But she had the distinct impression if she told Kelsey he couldn't sleep with her Joan would find a comfortable spot for him, probably right beside her. So she stuffed down her mutinous complaints and waited for Joan to vacate the room, something which only took a few minutes because she had to get ready for work.

"I swear I didn't know she would put us together," Kelsey said, holding his hands up in surrender to ward off Melly's advance. She didn't advance, though. She simply plucked the afghan and a pillow off the bed and tossed it onto the floor.

"What are you doing?" Kelsey asked.

"Making my bed," she said, arranging the afghan so it resembled a sleeping bag.

"Melly, c'mon, don't be like this. We're grown adults. We can safely share a bed."

She peered up at him from her vantage point on the floor, all hard-

103

bodied, perfect-featured 6'3" of him. "Yeah, I don't think so. I'll sleep down here."

Kelsey sighed, but he knew the argument was won. Melly had a look and a tone that indicated further protests on his part would be futile. At least he could gain control of one point. "You're not sleeping on the floor. I'll take the floor, I'm used to sleeping anywhere."

That was true, so Melly didn't argue. Kelsey had honed the ability to make himself fall asleep in any position as soon as he closed his eyes whereas she liked her creature comforts. She had never been able to sleep on the floor. "Thanks," she said, trying not to think this was yet another thing she owed him for. Instead she pulled the thick duvet off the bed and arranged a more comfortable pallet on the floor for him.

"You didn't leave yourself a lot of covers," he said. "If you get cold in the night…"

"Nope, not gonna happen, I am not inviting you to warm me up."

"You could have let me finish," he said, feigning irritability. "You know I hate to leave innuendo unfinished."

Melly laughed and stood, dusting her hands together as if she had finished manual labor instead of arranging comfortable cotton into a cushy bed. "Now what?"

"Now we do some recon," Kelsey said.

"Really?" she asked, eyes sparkling with excitement.

Kelsey smiled at her expression. "Why is that so exciting?"

"I don't know, it sounds sort of fun, like being a spy. I've always wanted a glimpse into what you guys do.

"If I'm James Bond, then that means you're my Bond Girl. Put on a bikini—I'll wait." He crossed his arms over his chest and leaned against the dresser. Melly remained expressionless, staring at him until he straightened again. "Geez, Melly, it's okay to play along sometimes. It was a joke."

Melly shook her head. "You're one of those give-an-inch-take- a-mile type people, Kelsey. If I give in and play along, you'll make me get wet and run down a beach while you take pictures, to make things feel authentic."

"Sometimes I hate how well you know me," Kelsey said. He put his hand to the small of her back and ushered her outside.

The rental car had a GPS, and Kelsey had apparently already looked up the addresses they would be visiting. Melly studied him while he typed them in, a no-nonsense expression on his usually jovial face. She was so perversely opposite from most women it was maddening. The jocular, frat-boy persona that charmed every woman Kelsey encountered did nothing for her. But this no-nonsense, responsible Kelsey was enough to make her leap across the console and kiss him senseless. If he opened his mouth and started talking about anything remotely serious, she was a goner.

"I'm starving," he said instead, and she sagged in relief.

"I know a great taco place," she said.

He quirked an eyebrow. "Will I have a stomach lining after I eat it?"

"I'm sure they make mild food for people with special needs—babies, old people, snipers, people like that."

"Remember I can't save your life if I'm locked in the bathroom screaming for death to come and end my suffering," Kelsey said.

She knew he wasn't exaggerating because the last time he ate peppers he called her at three in the morning requesting chicken soup. She had reluctantly gone to take care of him because he had no one else, and then he complained because the soup wasn't homemade. Recalling that story made her wonder why she was fighting a losing battle with attraction when he drove her crazy ninety percent of the time.

They migrated through another round of traffic jams that left Melly glad she had relocated to North Carolina. The slow pace of the south occasionally drove her crazy, but compared to the madhouse of California byways, it was heaven on earth. When they reached the taco stand, however, she felt a little nostalgic. She ordered in Spanish and the man answered her in kind. There had been no one to converse with in her native language since Jesus died. The smell of cilantro and habanero reminded her of her mother and, despite the heavy traffic, she felt suddenly homesick for the place where she grew up.

"That smells hot," Kelsey interrupted her nostalgia. "Are you sure I'm going to be able to eat this?"

"Don't be a baby. I got you the mildest stuff they had, I promise."

He followed her to the car, subdued. "I sort of liked it when you called me Babe before," he said. His tone was begrudging as if he was admitting a painful secret.

"I thought you didn't like endearments," Melly said.

"Not the ones you usually come up with, Schnookums, for instance. But Babe sort of sounded real. It was nice." He paused, his hands gripping the wheel, making no move to start the car. His gaze was focused on some distant point through the front windshield. "My therapist asked me if I'm in love with you."

"Here's your taco." She shoved the bag into his hands.

"Don't you want to know what I said?" he asked.

"No, because I know what you said. We're friends, and that's it."

He opened the bag and peered in. "Actually, I didn't answer."

They were sharing a soda. She took a sip and handed it to him.

"Your subtle avoidance cues tell me you don't want to talk about it," Kelsey said, shuffling the bag to his other hand so he could reach for the soda.

"There's a lot going on right now, Kelsey," Melly said.

"Is that why you don't want to talk about us?"

She didn't answer.

Kelsey sighed. "There are women who have literally camped outside my door to try and trap me into talking about our relationship. Why do you always have to be different, Melly?"

"Because I'm not crazy," she suggested.

"Well, there's that," Kelsey conceded. He simultaneously started the car and bit into a taco before putting the car in gear. They ate while he drove.

"Was it mild enough for you?" Melly asked when they arrived at their destination—a swanky-looking office building on the edge of town.

"Yes, it was perfect. I suppose you got the hot stuff."

"Only if you consider habaneros hot," Melly said.

He grimaced. "It's going to burn my lips when I kiss you."

"You're not going to kiss me," she assured him.

He leaned back giving her a smug smile. "Tell me you haven't been thinking about that kiss since it happened this morning."

"It was nice," she admitted.

"Nice?" he repeated. "It was awesome, and I think there should be many more of them in our future."

"We can't. I pinky swore."

"With Robert? Because I could see him doing something like that."

She was chagrined to realize she hadn't even thought of Robert as a reason to avoid him. "With Ashleigh."

"I should have known. What does PK have against us kissing?" Kelsey asked. "Is the rest of the world not allowed to have fun when she's around?"

"Stop trying to pretend you don't like Ashleigh when I know you do. Ashleigh was only trying to help. She knows I'm not the kind of woman who goes around kissing random men."

"I am not a random man."

"You know what I mean, Kelsey. I'm not that woman who can do things casually. I can't kiss someone and not have it mean anything."

He bit his lip, letting his fingers fiddle with the keychain dangling from the steering wheel. "What if it means something?"

"What are you saying?" she pressed.

"I'm saying maybe it's time we gave us a chance to be something more, Melly. I've hated being without you these last few months. I want you back in my life."

"I'll be back in your life. We'll go back to the way things were."

"I don't want things the way they were. I think I'm ready to take things to the next level. I want…I want to try us. Together."

His uncertain tone told her he hadn't thought things through. Like always, he was speaking from his heart with no help from his head. She couldn't fault him on it because at least he was being sincere, if not practical.

"Kelsey, I don't think that's a good idea," she said, being careful not to trample his feelings.

"Why not?" he asked, indignation and hurt mingling until he sounded like a pouting toddler.

"We're too different."

"Opposites attract," he countered.

"That only works in the movies," Melly said.

"Can I say one thing before we continue this discussion?" he asked. She nodded and he reached for her, kissing her with such exquisite tenderness and attention to detail she was the one clinging when he pulled away. "This isn't the movies, Melly; this is our life, and we're crazy attracted to each other. We always have been, even though you've tried to deny it."

"What?" The kiss wiped her mind as thoroughly as a concussion. It took a few seconds of Kelsey smiling at her to make her remember what they had been discussing. When she did, she pushed at his chest and eased out of his embrace.

"Fine, I'll admit it. We're attracted to each other. We have chemistry. Big, potent chemistry. But that's never what our problem has been about. The problem is the future."

"The future," he shifted. If he was wearing a collar, he would be tugging it right now. "Why do you always want to talk about that? Why can't we take it one day at a time?"

"Because that's not who I am. I need to know something has at least the possibility of a future before I go into it. I'm a forward thinker, Kelsey. I know you're not, and I know you resent the fact that I am, but these are the differences that make a relationship impossible."

"It's not impossible," he argued. "Okay, it's true I've made no secret of my desire not to get married and settle down any time soon. But I could see us together for the long haul, Mel. I could see us dating a few years and then, and then…" He couldn't bring himself to say the words. She could almost see his tongue swelling as the phrase "and then maybe we could get married" hung suspended in the back of his throat.

She decided to save them both and nip this insanity in the bud before it got any worse. "I want to have a baby before I'm thirty," she announced.

If she had stabbed him in the gut with a knife, he couldn't have looked more stunned or more horrified. "Thirty? You're almost twent- eight. That's two years away."

"I know. I'm not kidding around here, Kelsey. I want a home and family, and I want someone who is willing to provide them."

"Melly, that's crazy. You cannot meet someone, get married, and get pregnant in the next two years. Slow down the warp speed and think without using your hormones, woman."

"Don't tell me what to do. And what if I've already met the man?"

"You're not marrying Robert," he bellowed.

"Why not? Robert is nice, stable, and he shares my timeline."

"You don't love him," he thundered, the words filling the small space, echoing in the awful silence that followed. "Do you?" Kelsey added, his tone much softer.

"No. I don't love him. But maybe I could if I tried hard enough, if…" *If you would get out of my life long enough for me to try and forget you.* She drew her brows together and looked out the window. Maybe she did compare the men she dated to him, and maybe she did find them lacking. That was not a pleasant revelation, and it made her irrationally irritated with him. "Is this what recon is supposed to be about? Kissing and arguing?"

"On a good day, yes. And for the record, you're much more fun to kiss than Nick. His beard stubble leaves scratches." He rubbed at his cheeks and she laughed despite her anger. No one else had the power to evoke such a sweeping array of emotions in her. He picked up her hand and wove their fingers together. "Don't say no to us, Melly. Just think about it."

"It might surprise you to know I already have thought about it, Kelsey. A lot. That's what I do—I think about things endlessly before I make a decision. And as much as I care about you, I already know the idea of us together is a bad one. Unless you're willing to agree to a future."

"I want to," he said. "And I've never wanted to with anyone else. But I'm not there."

"I know, and that's okay. That's the beauty of our friendship. It's resilient. We'll go back to the way it was—no more kissing, no more talk of 'what if', just you and me and a whole lot of arguing." She smiled to soften any blow she may have unintentionally delivered to his ego.

Kelsey's return smile was half-hearted. He didn't want to go back to the way things were before, but neither was he ready to give up his independence. Melly was probably right because she usually was, and he had lost the heart to argue. They were at an impasse, but he couldn't help but feel like the roadblock was of their own making. One of them needed to unbend. Either she would have to give up her ridiculous timeline and quest for a decided future, or he would have to make a decided move toward commitment. The thought of being the one to give in left him feeling queasy. He definitely wasn't ready for that.

He faced front, staring at the building, already bored and tired of waiting for movement and action. The hardest part of any recon was waiting, but at least Melly was along for the ride this time. He rested his hand on her thigh and she didn't try to move it. If she thought he was going to stop touching her because they were resuming their friends status, then she was sadly mistaken. She turned to stare out the front windshield, too, and they began their watch in ponderous silence.

CHAPTER 11

"I'm going in."

The pronouncement startled Melly who was some-where between awake and asleep. They had been watching the building for what felt like forever in silence that should have been awkward after their big talk. Instead the quiet was cozy and intimate, if a little boring. "I thought you said we had to watch and learn first."

"We watched. I learned. I'm ready to go in."

"What could you possibly have learned?" Throughout the evening a handful of well-dressed people had entered and left the building. Melly had tensed each time, but none of them had been Charles.

"I learned if he's into something illicit, he's not conducting his business from here," Kelsey said. He bundled up their trash, packing it in the taco takeout bag.

"How do you know?" Melly asked.

"When someone is doing something bad, there's a heightened sense of paranoia, more security, possibly some hired thugs roaming around. The people who came and went today are all on the up and up."

"How can you tell?"

"Because I'm trained to be able to tell the good guys from the bad guys at a distance. If I had to pick someone to shoot today, I wouldn't have been able to find a target."

"Do you really make those kinds of decisions in the field? I thought you guys had assigned targets."

"Sometimes we do. Sometimes it's up to us to decide whose day it is to die." He sounded so nonchalant. Melly tried not to dwell on what they did, knowing the uncertainty and danger would gnaw at her. But seeing this side of him was a pleasant surprise with an unpleasant side effect—she had never been more attracted to him.

He glanced up and froze. "Keep looking at me like that, Melly, and I swear I'll kiss you again."

"I'm trying to remember why that would be a bad thing."

He grinned. "You're such a tease today. What's wrong with me that I like it?" He did kiss her then, a friendly buss on the cheek, and he was gone.

Kelsey left the car and walked purposefully toward the building. There was a reception desk in the main foyer. He tried to breeze by, but the woman sitting sentry hailed him back.

"Taco delivery for Mr. Tucker," Kelsey said, holding the bag aloft.

The woman picked up the phone. "I'll buzz someone to come get it."

"If it's okay, could I take it up?" Kelsey asked, attempting to use maximum self-deprecating charm. "I heard Mr. Tucker's a big tipper, and I could really use the cash." He flashed her a sheepish smile. She wavered, phone held uncertainly in the air. At last she set it down with a smile.

"Go on up, but don't tell them I let you through."

"Our secret." He gave her a wink and she giggled, which was disconcerting because she was Marilyn's age, old enough to be his mother. What was it with women and their never-ending susceptibility to flirtation? Except Melly, of course, who was exempt from every rule. No doubt if Melly had been the one behind the desk, she would have made the call and then had him ejected from the building. She roadblocked him at every opportunity. Why, then, couldn't he seem to get enough of her?

He took the stairs two at a time until he reached Charles Tucker's floor. It was near the top, which meant Charles Tucker was a bigwig. Not surprising since he had basically bought Melly's family. Kelsey guessed it was a safe bet he hadn't paid their social security or Medicare. All money had undoubtedly been under the table.

It was late, and the building was mostly empty. A lot of doors were closed, but a surprising amount were open with people still inside. Melly hadn't noticed their person of interest leaving, but that didn't mean he was there. He could have left before they arrived, or maybe he had never made it to work at all.

Kelsey scouted the hallway a few minutes and found the lack of security a joke. This man was running for the senate, and yet his personal security consisted of a few cameras in the hallway and a female gatekeeper who could be bought with a smile. At last he found the door he wanted and paused, craning his neck around the entry. Mr. Tucker's personal secretary had apparently left for the evening because the outer office was dark and deserted. There was a light on in the inner sanctum, drawing Kelsey's gaze like a laser beam. A man sat at his desk a couple of feet behind the nameplate that read "Charles Tucker." His head was down, his graying hair more salt than pepper, but even from this angle Kelsey could tell he was distinguished. His suit probably cost more than Kelsey's truck.

He eased through the door and slipped closer for further inspection. Charles didn't look up because Kelsey didn't make a sound. The inner office was fronted by glass, the glass covered by vertical blinds that were providentially open, allowing Kelsey to observe everything. He stood in the shadow created by the blinds, a few feet away from a man who had no idea he was being watched.

Charles looked up and tilted his neck back and forth as if trying to relieve a kink. His face was handsome and lined enough to add character without making him look old. Kelsey wondered if he'd had work done. His eyes were clear and blue, his hands well-manicured, the hands of a thinking man who takes good care of himself.

Kelsey's hands were now curled into fists. He hated the man as he had never hated anyone before. It didn't matter that he had treated

Melly kindly when she was a little girl, didn't matter that he had always been good to her family. All that was wiped away by his last act of betrayal. He had preyed on her, as sure as any criminal preys on someone young, innocent, and trusting. He could imagine what Melly had been like at seventeen—on the cusp of being as beautiful as she was now, filled with wide-eyed innocence and decency. She hadn't been prepared for a man who knew the ways of the world, hadn't been able to protect herself against his subtle advances. Charles Tucker had known exactly what he was doing by going after the underage daughter of immigrants, an orphan who lived in his home. If Melly cried foul, who would have believed her? No one. This man would have turned everything around and called her a liar.

Instead Melly had fled, pregnant and with a little brother to take care of. She had survived on her own, despite the odds, but she had lost something precious. Not only had she given up her first child, but she had lost her innocence and carried a burden of secret shame for years. Because of this man. And now she was being threatened again. Because of this man.

It would be so easy to kill him, and Kelsey had never been more tempted. He had never taken a life in anger. The few times he had killed a man, it had been because he was assigned to do so, because for some reason Nick couldn't complete the task and Kelsey had to take over. It had always been a rational, planned decision that calculated risk and effect. Never had he killed for anger or vengeance like he was considering now. It would be so easy. He knew how to erase security cameras. The woman downstairs was a witness, but all she had was a description of him. Five steps, snap his neck, and it would be done.

He also knew that what he was contemplating was murder, and it scared him. Perhaps he wasn't as far along in his therapy as he might have wished because he felt a little like he was having an out-of-body experience so many people with PTSD described. He retreated one step, then another and another until he was safely in the stairwell. Once there, he leaned against the wall sweating and shaking.

Melly would wonder what happened to him. She might come searching. That thought propelled him down the stairs and outside where he promptly lost his supper in the bushes. He straightened and jogged to the car.

He had hoped to slip behind the wheel and take off as if nothing was wrong, but that wasn't to be. Melly sat up, searching his face in alarm. "What is it? What happened?"

He shook his head.

"Kelsey, did you do something?"

He shook his head again. She continued to study him. He swiped the edge of his sleeve over his forehead, noting as he did so that his hands were still shaking. There was a little soda left in the cup, and he chugged it.

"Pull over," Melly commanded.

"I'm fine," he lied.

"Pull over," she repeated in that tone that probably made all twenty six of her kindergarteners snap to immediate attention. Kelsey was no different; he pulled into a parking lot and slid the gearshift into park. He didn't turn off the car, though; he needed to feel the cool air blasting on his face. "Look at me," Melly said. Again, Kelsey complied. She unlatched her seatbelt and leaned forward, cupping his face in her hands as she looked into his eyes.

He hoped she wasn't about to lecture him on what he had almost done or on how much help he still needed. "Ah, Kelsey," she said, letting her hands glide around him in a tight embrace. His panicky, sick feeling was covered by the feel of her softness pressed against him and by the scent of her hair tickling his nose. He closed his eyes and pulled her impossibly closer, crushing her, absorbing her stability.

"Is it worth it?" she whispered.

"What?"

"The job. Is it worth the mental anguish you're going through?" She eased away so she could see his face again. "Because you could get out. You could do anything, be anything. You're young, smart and talented. Don't feel trapped, because you're not." Her hands smoothed over his cheeks, and he smiled.

"Thanks for your vote of confidence." He took a breath, turning over her question in his mind. Was it worth it? The job wasn't a job; it was a total life commitment. Crazy hours with little time off, low pay, high danger, incredible stress. But it was also something most people in the world couldn't or wouldn't do. Didn't the necessity make it worthwhile? Still, her question bothered him and he didn't answer. Instead, he pressed his face to her neck and she soothed him, gently running her hand over his head, rubbing circles on his back, whispering gentle words in his ear. It was the type of attention he usually had to beg her for, and now she was offering it willingly because she knew he needed it. Melly could always see through to his heart, to know when he was sincere or not. And when he truly needed her, she was there.

Under her tender ministrations, his heart rate and breathing returned to normal, the cold sweats came to an end, and the nausea quelled.

"Want me to drive?" she whispered.

He was exhausted from his anxiety attack, but she was exhausted because it was past her bedtime in North Carolina, and they were here because she was the one with the problem, so he took a steadying breath and sat up.

"I'm fine, thanks." He was surprised by how close to true the words were. Either his sessions with Marilyn were helping, or there was a second option. Kelsey preferred to believe in that one. "You're magic, Melly."

"What are you talking about?" she asked, smiling as if he was teasing, but he wasn't.

"You have this effect on me, this soothing, restraining, tempering effect. I don't know how else to describe it but magic. You're one of the only people whose unsolicited advice I actually listen to. And when you touch me, it's, Melly…it's different than with everyone else." Why? Why was it different? The question had been on his mind a lot lately. His inability to find an answer was driving him crazy. What made Melly different from everyone else?

"You're introspective today, Jaws," Melly said. Her tone told him she wasn't sure how she felt about that. *Introspective* was usually the last word one would use to describe him. He wasn't a thinker; he was a doer.

"Therapy. Marilyn has me picking my life apart and thinking about everything, trying to figure out how it all fits together. The…the incident was harder for me because of my family dying. I never would have reached that conclusion on my own. The two didn't seem related." Now that he understood, though, he could see how Lolly's death had triggered all the anxiety and abandonment from his childhood. It's possible he had never dealt with his parents' passing until now, choosing instead to stuff everything down and put on a happy face.

"Is it helping?" Melly asked.

"I still feel weird about it, and I sort of feel like a failure for needing help in the first place, but it's helping. We've been doing this light therapy that seems like something from a sci-fi book. Basically she shines a bright light in my eyes, I move them back and forth and talk. But somehow I feel better when it's over. The dreams are getting better. I've been sleeping again. I stopped drinking, and I'm beginning to go an entire day without missing booze like it's a lover." He rested his hand on her leg. "Thanks, Melly. Thanks for pushing me to go when I needed it. I'm not sure what would have happened if you hadn't pushed."

"I thought it was Nick's ultimatum that made you go," she said.

"It was both. I didn't want to lose you. Would you have made good on your promise to never see me again?"

"I don't know," Melly said. "I felt like if I didn't get some space, then I might lose myself trying to fix you. It seemed best for both of us to take a step back." She reached over and rested her hand on his leg, smiling. "But I missed you, Babe."

Kelsey laughed. Even though she was using the requested endearment to tease him, something in his heart still flipped over, pretending it was real.

 elly fell into bed, exhausted. Kelsey did the same at his pallet on the floor. They didn't discuss what the morning would bring or what the day had brought. They simply curled up and fell asleep.

The next morning, Melly was awakened by the sound of Joan turning the knob on the bedroom door. By the time she had finished and pushed open the door, Kelsey was beside Melly, the duvet covering them both, his arms wrapped tightly around her.

"Oh, hey, Joan," he said, smiling up at her.

"Hey," Joan said, taking in their supposed sleeping arrangement with a frown of disappointment. Melly wondered if she had snooped, noticed the pallet on the floor, and attempted to catch them sleeping separately. Or maybe she truly had no idea of boundaries. Had she never heard of knocking?

"I have a short work day," Joan continued. "I was hoping maybe we could spend some time together." She zeroed in on Kelsey, ignoring Melly once again. What did she hope would happen? That Melly would magically disappear?

"Normally we would love to spend some time with you," Kelsey said, smoothly including Melly in the bonding time. "But we have a full agenda today. Sorry. Maybe you could let us buy you lunch before we go."

"Okay," Joan said. She lingered in the doorway, staring. Melly realized she looked exactly like someone who had been startled from sleep by a strange person in her bed—stiff, awkward, and held away from Kelsey at an angle. She relaxed and scooted closer, smiling. He resettled his arm around her and rested his cheek on hers.

"Have a good day," Kelsey added, hoping Joan might take it as the dismissal it was. She did, backing out of the room and closing the door as she went. Kelsey made no move to leave. Holding Melly first thing in the morning felt even better than he had imagined it might. He cinched her closer and pressed his face to her neck, inhaling. Her luxuriant hair tumbled over his face, smothering him with the scent of her shampoo.

"What was between you?" she asked.

"About ten feet and a whole lot of crazy. Did you see her eyes? She has stalker eyes; I can spot them a mile away," Kelsey said.

"No, I mean in high school. You dated for two years. Did you love her?"

He pulled away, smiling down at her. He loved that she was jealous. *Finally,* he wanted to say, but wisely refrained. For the last three years, he had flaunted a dazzling array of women in her face, and her reaction had been a bored yawn. Why was she jealous of Joan, his high school girlfriend? And how long could he draw out her jealousy, using it to feed the ego she had damaged so many times with her blatant dismissal and rejection?

But as he looked down into her face, beautiful even first thing in the morning with no makeup, he saw a trace of vulnerability that cut at him. He couldn't tease her. Not now, not about this. "Joan had a car," he admitted. "And a job. My grandma and I lived on a small pension. We weren't destitute, but there wasn't a lot of wiggle room. Joan drove me places and paid for dates. She bought me stuff. I used her. I liked her okay, but I never loved her."

"You're such a jerk, Kelsey," Melly whispered, but her voice, along with her eyes, were filled with a strange kind of tenderness and affection. "Such a shallow jerk." She tipped her face up and kissed him, a soft, slow, gentle kiss that was by far the most potent kiss he'd ever received. It took maximum effort to hold back, to not respond, but he instinctively knew allowing her to kiss him was a monumental step forward. Toward what end, he couldn't say. All he knew was that clutching her pillow and allowing himself to be kissed by her was a new level of pain and pleasure.

Melly was losing it at an alarming rate. She hadn't meant to kiss him, but his admission had caught her off guard. Gone was the cocky charmer who normally would have prolonged her torture, drawing out her jealousy for his own amusement. Instead he had readily confessed his sins and opened himself for her censure. She should have given it to him. Using Joan the way he used every other woman was a horrible thing to do. She should have lectured him on how to treat a lady. Instead she had kissed him. What was wrong with her? And, worse, she was still kissing him. But, once again, his reaction took her by surprise. She expected him to reciprocate. If he had, then she would have come to her senses and pushed him off, not just off her, but off the bed. But he hadn't reciprocated. He had closed his eyes and gone perfectly still, allowing her to take the lead, allowing her to kiss him to her heart's desire. And now she was in big, big trouble because she couldn't stop kissing him.

The curiosity and desire that had been mingling and building for three years was let loose and she had no idea how to stop, how to tell her hands to push at his chest instead of smoothing over his incredibly toned muscles. Have mercy, she was drowning.

In the end, Joan was her salvation. This time she did knock as she called through the door. "I realized I'm out of milk and juice. Sorry."

"S'okay," Kelsey called, clearing his throat a couple of times to get the words out. Joan went away and he rested his forehead on Melly's, both of them breathing hard. She knew he hoped she would kiss him again, but she had received the sting of mental clarity she needed. No way was she going down that rabbit hole again. As it was, they were both nearly undone. "And that was from kissing," Kelsey mused, noting their combined shortness of breath and stroke-level heart rates. "Imagine if we…"

She clapped her hand over his mouth. "No, let's not imagine anything else. You have to go now."

He smiled beneath her hand, kissing her palm. She jerked her hand away. "C'mon, Melly. Joan is leaving. We could…"

She jumped out of bed and out of reach before he finished the thought. Digging at her neck, she scrambled for the chain she always wore and pulled it from under her nightgown. Her fingers clutched reassuringly on the ring, and she held it aloft for his inspection. "There," she blurted, throwing out the word like a challenge.

Kelsey gave her a blank look. "What? Is this your not-so-subtle way of telling me you're a superhero? You put on the ring and turn invisible or something?" He was still giving her the smile, the one that said it was inevitable that she would come back to him and continue where they left off. She took another step back and bumped the dresser, glad for the pain that made a little more rational thought return to her brain.

"No, it doesn't make me invisible. It's a promise ring."

He scowled. "From the leprechaun?"

"It's not from Robert," she said. Hands shaking, she tucked it back into her nightgown and took a deep breath. "It's from me, to me. A promise I made myself that I would never repeat my past mistakes."

"I'm not following here," Kelsey said. He stretched, giving her a view of the ridges in his abdomen, all six of them.

"It's a, you know, a sort of purity ring," Melly said, blushing.

He blinked at her. "I see your lips moving, but the words don't make sense."

"This ring is a tangible reminder to hang on to my virginity."

His eyes narrowed in concern. "Melly, you've had a child. I'm sorry to disillusion you, baby, but you're not a virgin."

Tentatively, she stepped forward and perched on the edge of the bed. The ring had worked the way it was supposed to and the horrible temptation was fading. "There are two kinds of virginity—physical virginity and spiritual. I lost both, but I reclaimed the second, and I don't plan to lose it again."

"This sounds like the kind of bunk PK spouts," Kelsey said.

Melly didn't want to throw Ashleigh under the bus, but he was right. "Ashleigh and I have talked a lot. I told her how I messed up before, at least a little bit, and she sympathized. She told me how when she turned thirteen her dad gave her a ring to wear until she was married, one to remind her how cherished she was, how special. Ashleigh said whenever she was tempted, all she had to do was look at her ring and remember why she had chosen to wait until marriage—because it was worth it, because *she* was worth it. So I bought this ring, and I never take it off."

"Are you trying to tell me you believe in abstinence until marriage?" Kelsey said slowly, his tone somewhere between incredulous and mocking.

"Yes."

He laughed, clutching his stomach.

"It's not funny," Melly snapped.

"I'm not laughing at that. I'm laughing at all the energy I've waste being jealous of Robert. Poor schnook."

"Robert is not a schnook, and he respects my decision."

"Sure he does," Kelsey said, wiping his eyes. Sensing she was seriously angry, he sat up and reached out a hand, but she jerked away, avoiding his touch. He pressed forward anyway, clasping her hand and clutching it when she tried to get away.

"I get the whole waiting for the one, Melly, I do. Especially for you. Believe me; it makes me want to do a happy dance that you're not putting yourself out there with every guy who comes along. But waiting until marriage? Don't you think that's a little unrealistic, a little extreme?"

"Ashleigh did it," Melly pointed out, softened slightly by his sincere tone.

"But we both know she's not quite right in the head. You, though, you're normal."

In an uncharacteristic and mercurial mood shift, Melly leaned close and slipped her arms around his neck, resting her head on his shoulder. "You have to understand how it was after the last time, Kelsey. The sense of failure, guilt, and shame was overwhelming. I let everyone down, my parents' memory, Jesus, the Tuckers, myself. I have lived with the shame every minute of every day since I first realized I was pregnant. I felt like I was drowning in it. I decided after that not to be with anyone unless I was sure I loved him, but that wasn't enough to make the feelings go away. And then I took it another step and decided to hold out for marriage. Since then, I've felt whole again, hopeful."

He smoothed his hand gently down her back, her silky soft hair tickling his palm. "But abstinence is so...abstinent."

Melly chuckled. "That's kind of the point."

"I mean it seems like taking things to the most extreme."

"That's because sex is extreme. How did it become so casual? I'm the worst case scenario of what can go wrong."

"Not every encounter produces an unwanted pregnancy," he said.

"It wasn't unwanted. It was unplanned and impossible, but never unwanted. Maybe an all-or-nothing lifestyle doesn't make sense to you, but it does to me. I'm waiting until I'm married, the end."

"I'm really starting to hate PK. She's ruining my life."

"You don't hate Ashleigh. You love her, and so do I. Her friendship has helped me heal in a lot of ways. She was there every single day after Lolly died. Every single one, without fail. Even when I tried to push her away, she wouldn't go. She kept showing up. Finally I started to function again, to believe I might make it through."

"Melly, I'm sorry," Kelsey said. He shifted, placing his arms around her as he drew her against his chest. "I should have been there. I should have been the one piecing you back together."

"Kind of hard to do when you were falling apart yourself," Melly said. "You were in a free fall; we both were. Let's forgive each other and move on. What's on today's agenda?"

This, he thought. He could gladly stay exactly where he was and hold her all day, content to have her near him with her guards down. A soft and vulnerable Melly was more potent than anything he had ever encountered. His hand slid over her, arcs of electricity stinging his palm. "Today we make contact."

Melly tensed. "With whom?"

"With everyone. First we start with Anna and her family to warn them. Then we begin the process of drawing out whoever is threatening you." Now he was tense. He didn't like the idea of exposing her and putting her in harm's way. If there was any other way to do it, he would. But using her and forcing the issue was the most expedient way to find resolution. He had no time or patience for a game of cat and mouse.

"I guess we'd better go," Melly said. She sounded as reluctant as he felt. There was no tension in her, none of her usual reserve. Previously she always held herself slightly away, but not this morning. Today she was draped on him, letting him experience all her velvety softness as her curves molded to his hard planes. It was sensory overload, almost but not quite too much to handle. He smoothed his lips back and forth on the top of her head, inhaling her scent, adding to the potent mix. If he closed his eyes, he could pretend they woke like this every morning, that they had the sort of life together where they went to bed in each other's embrace and woke the same way. He didn't hate that vision, didn't hate it at all.

They lingered for another moment because, despite everything, the moment was perfect. Kelsey was tempted to try again, to plead a case for them as a couple, but begging a woman to be with him was new, and he didn't like the sensation. Maybe he was as shallow as Melly had always accused him of being because he couldn't ever remember another time a woman had said no to him. What if that was what this was about? What if he wanted to be with her because she was the ultimate challenge and always had been?

Melly gathered her belongings to take her turn in the bathroom while Kelsey was left with his newly deep and disturbing thoughts. No, he decided. It wasn't that Melly was a challenge. They had three years of solid friendship to dispel that notion. She had always been a challenge he had wanted to conquer, but in an abstract sort of way. This was different; this was definitive, and it scared him.

As he had told first Nick and then Ashton, they were only twenty-seven years old. In two weeks, he would be twenty-eight, but that was still too young for what he was contemplating, for what Nick and Truck had already done. Had they never heard the divorce rate before? Did they not understand most relationships failed? Didn't they realize they were giving up their freedom years before it was necessary? Sure, no one wanted to see an old man ogling young women and serial dating. But Kelsey had another decade at least before he would even reach his prime, let alone surpass it. The longer he stayed single, the longer he wanted to stay single. Forty seemed like a good time to settle down.

But then there was Melly. In all his life, Melly was the only woman who had ever touched his heart. She challenged him not only to step up his game, but to be a better man. He liked the person he was when he was with her. If he were being honest, he would admit when he pictured the someday future mother of his children, she looked a whole lot like Melly. But not now. He could not, *would* not concede this one point, not now, not ever. He wasn't ready to settle down, and that was that.

But Melly was. What would it feel like to see her with someone else? To sit at her wedding and watch her marry another man. To go to the hospital and watch her hold another man's baby.

He stood and began to pace the small room. No way. Over his dead body would that happen. Maybe she would wait for him to be ready. A derisive little laugh escaped on a puff of air, and he shook his head. Melly had already made clear she had no intention of waiting for him to get his act together, and Melly always said what she meant. For once, he wished she had been playing a game to trap him, but she hadn't. She had been telling him like it was so he wouldn't be disillusioned when things didn't work out between them, sparing him from heartache before it could begin.

Melly returned while he was still stewing in his anger and misery. He grasped her biceps and gave her a little shake. "I will not be an usher at your wedding," he declared.

"The bathroom's all yours," she said, unfazed by his odd mood change. She watched as he stormed around the room, gathering supplies.

"Maybe you could leave me the number of your therapist. I think she and I could have a meaningful conversation while you're gone."

"Stay away from Marilyn. I don't want you planting ideas in her head." He had the paranoia that if Melly and Marilyn ever got together, he would soon spend his therapy sessions discussing his deep-rooted fear of commitment. Melly's bubbling laughter followed him down the hall and by the time he reached the bathroom he was smiling. No doubt about it—the woman made him crazy.

CHAPTER 13

Melly's laughter was gone by the time Kelsey was finished getting ready. He grabbed a toaster pasty from Joan's kitchen, but Melly said she wasn't hungry.

She was quiet as they drove, and he left her to her thoughts, knowing she was probably too tense for idle chitchat. "Ready for this?" he asked when they pulled up in front of the house that contained her daughter.

"Not in a million years," Melly said.

"C'mon," Kelsey urged. "Now or never."

Never, Melly thought. Her stomach was queasy, even though she hadn't eaten anything to make it rebel. Kelsey took her hand as they left the car, giving it a reassuring squeeze. They ascended the porch together and Kelsey rang the bell. Melly resisted the urge to hide behind him and poke her head out like a shy toddler.

The door cracked open and Melly's daughter peeked out. She must have judged them safe because after her first cautious glance, she opened the door wider and stepped into the gap. "Yes?" She looked and sounded so much like Melly it was uncanny, though there was a little of Jesus in her features, too. Her hair was as long and silky as Melly's, swinging to the middle of her back in a thick braid. Her eyes

127

were the same shade of black with thick fringes of lashes over each, and she even had the same deep dimple in her right cheek. Melly's mouth worked up and down a few times but no sound came out. Kelsey prepared to fill the silence, but she at last found her voice.

"Is your m-mother home," she asked, her voice a hoarse whisper.

Anna nodded. "Just a minute." She disappeared and left the door gaping. "Mom, it's for you," she called. A few seconds later, the woman Melly had met for a few minutes ten years ago stepped into view. Recognition flashed across her features, and Melly knew the other woman was experiencing the worst kind of dread at her appearance. She quickly stepped outside and banged the door loudly closed.

"What do you want?" she asked, trying to sound brave but failing miserably. Melly hated the fear and anguish in her voice. "If you're here for money..." she let the thought trail off, looking helplessly around.

"No, please, it's not like that," Melly said. "I needed to get in contact with you, and this is the only way I knew how. I'm sorry for showing up and startling you. I wouldn't if it weren't an emergency."

"An e-emergency," the woman stammered. She wiped her eyes though she didn't appear to be crying. Maybe she was trying to urge her eyes not to overflow.

Melly nodded and took a breath. "I received a threat about Anna, about your daughter. Her father is somewhat famous right now and..." she broke off, realizing she was bungling things badly.

"I thought you said you didn't know who her father was."

"I lied." The woman blanched, and Melly hastened to continue. "I couldn't tell him about the baby for a lot of reasons. But he would never try to gain custody. If he had known about the baby, he would have been relieved by the adoption. For reasons I won't go into, he wouldn't want anyone to know about her." She took another breath. Now wasn't the time to try and keep things hidden. "The father is Charles Tucker." Melly hastened on, trying not to let the woman's startled reaction bother her. "As you know, he's running for senate. I received a letter threatening me not to tell anyone about her. The letter threatened to hurt Anna, I mean your daughter, if I told anyone.

I wanted to make sure you're aware and do whatever is necessary to protect her."

"So you're not here to try and take her back?" The woman's lip quivered and this time her eyes did fill with tears.

"Of course not," Melly said. "I would never do that. I've always wanted what's best for her. She looks happy and well settled. I would never want to disturb that. You know I live in North Carolina now. I have a life there, I have friends and family." She glanced up at Kelsey and he smiled down at her, reaching out to put his arm around her shoulders in a show of support. The bracing feeling of his arm gave her a much-needed boost of strength. "I teach kindergarten, and I know how important a stable, loving home is. I simply wanted to let you know about this situation. I'm sorry I scared you."

The woman nodded, her eyes still wide and filled with worry.

"I'll go now," Melly added. She started to turn away, but the woman hailed her back.

"Wait, Mellisandra."

Melly paused and turned back.

"I never got the chance to thank you for what you did. You can't know what it's meant…we tried so hard for so many years to have a baby, and we tried other adoptions, too. She's the joy of our lives, so bright, beautiful, and sweet. We told her about you. I mean, we both have fair skin and blond hair, so it's not like we could keep the adoption a secret, but we never wanted to. We've only told her good things about you, how much you loved her, how much you wanted to keep her but couldn't. Would it be okay if we tell her you're a teacher? Give her something to aspire to."

"I would like that," Melly said. Her voice quavered and she cleared her throat.

"I think someday she'll want to come find you. We support that decision; we'll support her in whatever she decides."

Melly nodded, secure in the knowledge she had made a good match for her daughter. "Thank you for taking such good care of her. Maybe someday we'll meet again."

The woman nodded, smiling now. Kelsey put his arm around Melly again and led her away.

"You okay?" he asked.

She nodded. "I really am. Before now I could only hope that this was the right decision. Now I see it was." She turned once more and looked at the house. It wasn't grand, but it was comfortable. A playhouse was in the back yard, along with a dog that was frisking around, barking. Anna was happy; Anna was loved. What more could any mother want for her child?

Kelsey cupped her face in his hands, smiling down at her. "She looked and sounded exactly like you, Mel. She's going to grow up to be a stunner. I hope we meet her before then so I can stand in line to help keep the boys away."

Melly clutched his shirt and smiled up at him, pleased by the sweet sentiment. "I would like that, I would like you to meet her someday."

There was a loud cracking sound and Kelsey threw Melly on the car, his body plastered over her. His eyes scanned the horizon, his posture tense and ready.

"Was that a gun?" Melly whispered.

"Yes, but it was far away and a low caliber. I don't think it was aimed at us. Probably kids shooting tin cans." He gave her a self-deprecating smile. "It's possible that I'm wound a little too tight right now."

"You think?" Melly said, but she was smiling. Perhaps it had been an overreaction on his part, but she was heartened to know how seriously he took their safety. "I thought maybe this is the way you end every date, the full Kelsey Adams treatment."

"You said I can't give you the full treatment until you're married," he reminded her.

That made her blush, which made him smile. "Can we get up now?" She could only imagine what her daughter's mother was thinking if she was watching through her window.

Kelsey stood and helped her up. "Are you okay? I didn't bash your head or give you whiplash, did I?"

She shook her head. How could he have injured her when he

cradled her body to protect it from impact? Her cheeks felt traitorously warm again, and she turned away. "What now?" she asked.

"Now we go cut the head off the snake," he said.

She didn't know what that meant, and she was too tired and drained to figure it out. Kelsey was tense as he wended his way through the city, parking in almost the same spot they had used the night before. They stared up at the office building, squinting when the sun gleamed hard off the windows.

"Are you going to pretend to deliver tacos again?" she asked. She didn't feel comfortable with him going back today after his close encounter with a breakdown the night before.

Kelsey shook his head. "I'm not going in this time; you are."

"You want me to go in there?" Melly knew she sounded afraid, and she hated that. She bit her lip to stop more words from pouring out. She hadn't seen Charles in ten years, since the day she found out she was pregnant and left his house. She never wanted to see him again, and she certainly wasn't prepared to do it today. What if she hadn't grown as much as she thought she had over the last decade? What if she took one look at his handsome, distinguished face and fell in love with him all over again? What if she had never stopped loving him?

"I wouldn't do it if it wasn't absolutely necessary, but I need to see his reaction to you, need to see if it's genuine so I can know if he's the one behind the threats."

Melly nodded, trying to look brave and stoic. What happened to all her defenses? She used to be so good at using them. Now she was stripped bare, laid emotionally naked for Kelsey's inspection, and she couldn't seem to mind. It was then she realized how much she had come to trust him, to depend on him. Theirs was no longer a one-sided relationship with her as the caregiver and him as the taker. It was a relationship of equals. She put that thought away for later inspection, too overwhelmed to hash out its meaning now.

"You won't be alone, Mel, it will only feel that way. I'll be there, watching, even if you can't see me, okay?"

She nodded. He told her where Charles' office was and what he wanted her to do. He watched her go and pulled out his phone, placing a call to the secretary whose name and number he had memorized.

"Hi, is this Wanda Llewellyn?" he asked, knowing full well it was. "This is Cardinal Flower Shop. We have a delivery for you, but, this is so awkward, you'll really have to forgive us. Our delivery guy tripped and sprained his ankle as soon as he stepped out of the truck. He asked us to give you a call to see if you'd be willing to pop outside and retrieve them? I'm so sorry to ask. Jerry's getting up in years, and we should really get someone else, but, anyway, you don't need to hear all this. Forget it; I'll have him drive back and deliver the roses myself. What time do you leave today?"

She interrupted, hastening to assure him that she would be happy to step outside and retrieve her flowers. Kelsey would have smiled at how well his ruse worked if he didn't feel bad for the lie. Poor Wanda thought she was getting roses when what she was really getting was the runaround. He gave her the description of a minivan parked in front of the office—praying it wasn't hers—and then he entered the building.

He wasn't as good at ghosting as Lolly had been. No one was. If Melly's little brother had been there, no one would have seen him slip through the service entrance. As it was, two people saw Kelsey, but he put on his I'm-supposed-to-be-here expression, a combination of cheerfulness and determination. That, combined with his all-American surfer-boy looks, usually worked to grant him access wherever he wanted to go. He was too wholesome-looking for anyone to believe he was up to no good, which made him glad he was one of the good guys. With his looks, charm, and finely-honed skills, he could be a world-class criminal.

After his initial encounter near the door, he made it to Charles Tucker's office undetected, behind Melly whose posture was that of someone walking to the guillotine. Her head was up, her expression determined, her steps purposeful if somewhat plodding. *You can do this, Mel,* he wanted to tell her. *You're stronger than you know.* He was constantly amazed by her. If this morning he had been confronted by the daughter he gave up ten years ago, he would have dissolved into a weeping mess, throwing himself on her front porch in a display of nerves and grief. But Melly hadn't flinched, hadn't given herself away, hadn't thrown her arms around her daughter and yelled "I'm your mother!" Instead she had handled the situation with class and dignity, the same way she did everything.

Thanks to his ruse, Wanda-the-secretary was absent from her post, allowing Melly to walk right in to the inner sanctum. This morning Charles Tucker's door was closed. She paused before it, took a deep breath, and knocked. Kelsey positioned himself so he could see and not be seen. Charles told her to enter, and the show began.

Melly opened the door and took a step inside, leaving the door wide open. Kelsey hadn't told her to do that, but she must have realized he would need to see and hear her. Charles' head was down as he finished whatever he was working on. He probably expected to see his secretary. It was a safe bet to say he didn't expect to see Melly. She didn't say a word, didn't make a move, merely stood there, hands clenched tightly into balls as she waited for him to look up.

When at last he did, his debonair smile gave way to shock Kelsey thought was genuine. Melly was definitely the last person he expected to see that day. If he was the one blackmailing her, he certainly didn't expect her to come and confront him. His face turned ashen, his mouth went slack. For a second, Kelsey wondered if maybe he was having a heart attack. But he didn't clutch his left side. He simply blinked, trying to make sure the beautiful woman now standing in front of him was real.

"Melly," he whispered. Kelsey had the feeling Charles wasn't one to reveal his emotions. If he was a politician, he was probably good at wearing a mask. But today his mask was gone, and his feelings were on display. What he felt for Melly seemed to be a combination of reverence and affection. If he had simply remained a father figure, Kelsey would have been heartened by the sincere feeling in his tone. But since Kelsey had knowledge of the twisted inner workings of his heart, he was repulsed.

Charles slowly stood and came around the desk, arms

outstretched, and Kelsey's control snapped. He made his presence known, stepping into the office and inserting himself between them.

"Don't," he said, his voice full of steel, his fists barely contained in their quest to seek vengeance.

Charles stopped short and looked at him in surprise, but his mask recovered more quickly this time. "Hello," he said. "Are you a friend of Melly's?" Not waiting for an answer, he tried to sidestep Kelsey to get to Melly again, but Kelsey pivoted, intercepting him again.

"You are this close to meeting your maker, and I swear if you touch her, I will kill you."

Charles stopped short again, a perplexed frown on his face. "I'm not sure who you think you are, young man, but Melly and I are old friends. We go way back. I haven't seen her in some time, and I would like to give her a hug."

"I'm sure you would," Kelsey said, letting all his disgust seep into the words. "But you're not touching her ever again. I know what you did to her, you sick…" he broke off, editing himself for Melly's sake. "Stay right there because if you think I'm kidding about killing you, then it will be the last mistake you ever make."

Either he believed what Kelsey was saying, or he was too stunned to advance because he stopped short, craning his neck around Kelsey to see Melly. "Melly, what's this about? You haven't seen me in ten years, and you bring this man to threaten me? That's not like you." He frowned his disapproval as if he were Melly's long-lost father. Kelsey wanted to throttle him, but Melly laid a restraining hand on his forearm.

"I'm not here to threaten you, Charles. I'm here to find out why you've threatened me," Melly said. Her voice sounded so strong and sure. Kelsey knew it was a sharp contrast to the way she was feeling on the inside, and he was proud of her for her bravado.

"Threatening you?" Charles asked. His indignation seemed genuine, but Kelsey couldn't be sure because his politician's mask was now firmly in place. "My dear, why would I threaten you? I haven't seen you in so many years." He smiled. "It's good to see you again, Melly. Really good. How's Jesus?"

"He's dead," Kelsey blurted, saving Melly the pain of saying the words. Charles had the decency to blanch and turn away.

"What happened?" Charles asked. "Did he get caught up in a gang? I know that was always a worry for you."

"No," Kelsey answered again as if Melly wasn't there. He didn't want her talking to this man unless she had to. "He died with honor as a United States Marine. He was part of a scout sniper unit; he was the best at what he did, the best man I've ever known, thanks to Melly and her influence on him."

Charles scowled at him. "Calm down, son. I'm not sure why you're so angry, but Melly and I are old friends. I've known her since she was a toddler."

That was almost Kelsey's undoing. He could picture himself reaching out to deck the old man across the jaw, hopefully shattering it into a million pieces. The only thing that stopped him was the fact that, despite how well-maintained he was, the man *was* old. Kelsey didn't like people who didn't fight fair, and clobbering this man—though satisfying—would in no way be a fair fight.

"I'm not your son," he said instead. "And I know all about your friendship. You should have gone to prison for what you did to her."

Charles was beginning to look ashen again. "Now hold on there. I'm afraid there's been some misunderstanding." He looked at Melly, trying to appeal to her again. "I'm sorry if you got the wrong impression, Melly." His gaze settled on Kelsey again with a sickening amount of we're-men-and-all-females-are-melodramatic cronyism. "She was a young, impressionable girl, and I was a father figure to her. I'm not sure what she told you, but I think you have the wrong idea."

If Charles didn't know about the baby, then he had no idea a DNA test of their child was all that was needed to dispel his lie. Kelsey itched to tell him, but he knew nothing would be made better by revealing Melly's secret if he didn't already know.

"We have proof of the affair," he said instead. A bead of sweat broke out on Charles' lip.

"Melly, why are you doing this?" Charles said. "I was good to you. We were friends."

"You were good to me, and we were friends until you took advantage of that friendship," Melly said. "I was a seventeen-year-old orphan, Charles. I had Jesus to look after, nowhere to go, and my parents had died. You used my vulnerability. You used *me*. You took what was a pure and innocent friendship between us and turned it into something twisted."

"And now you're here to exact revenge," he said. "You come to my office and make threats, after all I did for you, after all I did for your family." He shook his head as if he was disappointed in her, and then he reached into his pocket. "How much will it take to make this go away? I assume this is about money. It always is."

"Maybe for you," Kelsey said. "But Melly's not like that. She's good, and honest, and respectable."

"Then why are you here?" Charles asked, his voice going flat with renewed anger and impatience.

"Because someone is threatening her," Kelsey said. He took a step closer until he towered over Charles. His voice dropped to a menacing whisper. "And if I find out it was you, they won't be able to put you back together when I'm finished."

Charles swallowed hard, his Adam's apple bobbing erratically. "Are you threatening me? I'm a candidate for the senate. I'll have your job, marine."

He must have deduced that Kelsey was a marine, or else it was a lucky guess from his statement about Lolly. Kelsey smiled, and it must have been terrifying because Charles blanched again. "Go ahead. Then we'll find out the statute of limitations in California for statutory rape. That would play really well in your campaign."

"She was eighteen," Charles hissed, no longer trying to pretend nothing happened.

Kelsey shook his head. Melly was eighteen when she had the baby, but seventeen when she got pregnant. All that was needed was the DNA test, and they would have the proof they needed.

"She told me she was eighteen. Not my fault she lied," Charles said. He tugged at his collar, the cool and in control business mogul gone and replaced by this worm of a man who was on the verge of begging for mercy.

"Doesn't matter what she said, only matters what she was. And you admitted you knew her since she was a toddler. You watched her grow up. You knew exactly how old she was."

"She enticed me. She was a tease."

Kelsey didn't know he was going to hit him until he took a swing, but Melly did. She simultaneously lunged for his arm and shoved Charles out of the way, ducking in time to miss taking the blow herself.

"We're leaving now," she said, shoving at his chest. In his blind rage, he barely felt her hands pushing him out of the office.

"Why didn't you let me finish him?" he asked as soon as she was able to herd him out the door and to the stairwell.

"Because I didn't want to watch you throw away your career for the satisfaction of breaking his nose. It's not worth it."

"It is to me. That guy is..." he grimaced, unable to find a description evil enough for how much he hated the man.

"Yes, he is," Melly agreed. She sounded subdued. She hooked her arm through his and tugged, leading him down the stairs. She felt good about her reaction to Charles. She didn't love him anymore, maybe she never had. She'd had a certain amount of awe and hero worship for him, but that was gone now. All she had felt for him this time was a whole lot of disgust and a little bit of pity.

"He couldn't have my career without indicting himself," Kelsey pointed out.

"You underestimate how vindictive and sneaky the rich and powerful are. I grew up in this world, and I know how they work, even if I was only the daughter of the hired help. He would have had your job, and he would have remained squeaky clean." He still might. She had seen the impotent rage in Charles' eyes. He didn't like letting someone else win. Being cowered by the younger and larger Kelsey had definitely been a loss. As much as she didn't want to involve Anna or her family, they were her ace in the hole. She would have the DNA test if it meant keeping Kelsey in the marines and out of the brig.

They settled in the car. Kelsey gripped the steering wheel. He was still shaking with rage. He reached for the ignition, but she put her hand on his arm.

"Kelsey, I can't have you wandering around San Diego as a loose and lethal canon. We've done what we needed to do; let's go home."

He took a breath and tried to pull himself together. If it was anyone but Melly witnessing his mental collapse, he would have been mortified. He would have laughed it off, covering his near losses of control with a joke. But this was Melly who cared about him unconditionally and who understood what he was going through.

"I'm okay, Melly, even if it looks like I'm not. In a weird way, these little episodes are sort of a good sign. Better than sweeping all my feelings under the rug and drowning my emotions in jokes or malt liquor. In fact, Marilyn's going to be downright proud when I tell her how I almost killed that guy twice in one weekend. She might declare me cured."

Melly laughed, more a release of nerves than actual amusement. She remembered what Shelby had told her about how Kelsey had exploded when they landed at the hospital in Germany, how he had shielded Jesus's body and attacked the orderlies who tried to take him away.

At her request, Shelby had told her everything. The guys were under the seal of confidentiality; their assignments were classified. But Shelby was a civilian and free to discuss whatever she wanted. Melly had never asked about any of their missions before, but she needed to know what Jesus's final hours were like. She was glad he had died as he would have wanted—in the line of duty, surrounded by his team. He had loved Nick, Ashton, and Kelsey as much or more than he had loved her. In them, he had seen the real life superheroes he dreamed about as a child. He wanted nothing more than to be one of them, to be off saving the world somewhere. He died as he had lived—with honor and integrity, a hero.

Though she would never have wished her brother's death, Melly could also see the good that was springing from it. His loss had forced her and Kelsey to confront things that had eaten away inside of them for decades. She had changed for the better, letting go of old guilt and shame, finding peace over her decision to give up Anna. She had let down her barriers, opening herself to Ashleigh's friendship, as well as the care and concern of her family and their church. For so long, she had been alone with only Jesus and his team as her companions. Now her life was rich with friends she counted as family.

Kelsey was changing, too. He was becoming the man Jesus had always insisted he was—loyal, responsible, selfless, mature, caring. Jesus would have loved the changes. Melly loved the changes.

"Uh-oh," she said as that last thought swirled around her head and took root.

"What?" Kelsey asked. He seemed to have regained his equilibrium. He wasn't quite smiling, but he looked relaxed once again.

She stared up at him, transfixed by his stunning good looks, horrified. He glanced at her and did a double take.

"Melly, what is it? You look like you're going to toss your cookies."

She felt like it, too. She doubled over, the air leaving her lungs in a rush as she crossed her arms over her midsection. To the outside observer, she appeared to be giving herself the Heimlich. Maybe she should; she certainly felt like she was choking.

"What is it?" Kelsey pressed. He laid a concerned hand on her back.

"I think I'm in love with you."

For a second he was nonplussed, and then he smiled. "This is news why? You've been in love with me since we met."

She shook free of his hand and gave it a shove. "No, *you've* been in love with you since we met. This is definitely new." *And disastrous.* She squinched her eyes closed and rocked back and forth. How could she be so stupid and self-destructive to fall for someone with whom she had no future? True, Kelsey had changed, but not that much. Not enough. She had no delusions about the outcome of them attempting a romance together. It would end, maybe amicably or maybe badly, but it would definitely end. They wanted different things. They weren't on the same page, and they never would be.

"Baby, this is a good thing," he said.

She turned sad, solemn eyes on him. He rested his hand on her leg and gave it a little shake.

"Think about it—you and me, together. I know you think I wasn't thinking clearly last night when I said I wanted us to be together, but I was. It's a new day. I've had hours to think about it, and I still feel the same. I want to be with you, Melly, really be with you, only you. You think I'm some sort of shallow serial dater, and, maybe this is a cliché, but it's only because they weren't you. I'll be committed to you and only you."

She didn't doubt his sincerity or his potential for commitment. What she doubted was his ultimate goal. "And what about the fact that I won't be with anyone until I'm married?"

He frowned but in a perplexed kind of way, more annoyance than true regret. He lifted the hand on her leg and waved it as if clearing the air between them. "I get it—you're saving yourself until you're in love. But you said you're in love with me." He turned the full power of his potent smile on her. "Problem solved."

She bent over again, touching her forehead to her knees with a groan. "Kelsey, that's not what I said at all."

"But it's what you meant, and I agree. I've been too lax in that area. It should be reserved for something special, for love." He sounded almost shy now, which made her feel even worse. Was he trying to say he loved her, too? He didn't need to; she already knew. She had always known the potential was there. For that reason, she had been careful with him, not wanting to do anything to tweak him in her direction, to nudge him into falling in love with her. Dummy her—she hadn't ever foreseen herself falling for him. And yet here she was.

"No, Kelsey, I'm not saving myself for love. I'm saving myself for marriage. *Marriage.*" He smiled again, patronizingly this time as if he was sure he could coax her to change her mind. The trouble was, he probably could. But she didn't want him to. "Are you proposing?"

The wheel jerked as he glanced sharply in her direction again. "What? No. You know how I feel about that."

"And you know how I feel about abstinence. You're not listening to me."

"But, Melly, it doesn't make sense."

"Like your odd aversion to commitment doesn't make sense to me."

"I don't have an aversion to commitment, at least not to you. I'm saying I want to be with you, only you, in a long term relationship."

"Define long term," she said.

He started to sweat. "What do you mean? Why do we have to define it? No one starts dating with a set wedding date."

"No, but people do start dating with similar expectations of the outcome. I want marriage. You don't. The end."

He shook his head. "Would you listen to you? You're being stubborn."

It was either pummel him or laugh. She chose laughter.

He smiled and reached for her hand. "Seriously, Melly, you're being your usual stringent self on this one. Chill out. Go with the flow."

"I would if it was anything less important. But this is too big and it means too much to me. I've always had the dream in my head of the handsome prince of a husband, the home, and the two and a half kids. Nowhere in that story did the prince say 'We could stick it out for a while. I could probably stop dating other women if I set my mind to it.'"

He ignored her barb and focused on the first part of her statement. "Every girl has that dream, Melly. Not every girl gets it."

"Because they give up too easily," Melly said.

Kelsey laughed. "I've never heard you cocky before. What makes you sure you'll get it when so many others have given up?"

She pressed her fingers to her temples. "I don't think I can talk about this anymore."

Kelsey smiled again, sure he was wearing her down. This time she couldn't quite resist the urge to pummel him. She reached out and slugged his shoulder. "Shut up," she said.

"I didn't say a word."

"I know what you're thinking."

His brows knit together. "Perhaps the us dating plan has a downside I didn't count on. No one knows me better than you."

It didn't have a downside; it had a cliff so steep that to plunge off it would be certain death, but she didn't say so. She was too empty to talk about it again. Later, when they were home and the current nightmare was over, she would try and explain it to him again.

CHAPTER 14

"What are we doing here?"

They sat in front of the home where Melly spent much of her childhood, the home where her parents had worked, the home where she had become pregnant with Anna.

"We're here to continue phase one of our directive: surprise attack. Come on." Kelsey got out of the car, but Melly remained.

"I can't go in there," she said.

He studied her, deciding how best to handle her. "You're Melly Garcia. You can do anything," he said at last.

"Not this. I can't confront Diana Tucker this way after what I did to her family."

"You were as much a victim as she was. Besides, we don't have to bring any of that up. We'll pop in to say hello and observe her reaction to you."

Reluctantly, she stepped from the vehicle and allowed him to lead her to the front porch. This time she did hover behind him as he rang the bell and waited. A Mexican woman opened the door. She must have been new to the country because it was clear she didn't speak much English. Melly stepped forward and, in Spanish, asked to see

Diana. She hoped Diana would be at one of her various clubs or committees—the woman was hardly ever home. Of course it was their luck she was home on this day.

The maid showed them to the formal sitting room and told them to have a seat while she retrieved Diana. Melly's mind flew back to all the times her mother had performed this same ritual. Answer the door, greet the guests, show them inside, find the lady of the house. She felt another stab of nostalgia, quickly followed by remorse. While it was true Diana had never felt as warm or familial as Charles and could occasionally throw a temper tantrum, overall she had been kind and fair. She had agreed to take Melly and Jesus in, the same as her husband. She had even taken Melly shopping and had her hair done. Child or not, victim or not, Melly had betrayed that kindness in the worst possible way, and she couldn't be more sorry. But it also wasn't as if she could start off with an apology. What if Diana didn't know? Melly would be doing more harm than good with her need to confess and find absolution. Kelsey was right; if she could successfully get through this visit, there was nothing she couldn't do. Facing all her old demons and past mistakes in one fell swoop was daunting, to say the least.

"Melly," Diana said. Her heels clicked on the cool tile as she entered the room, arms outstretched. Melly stood and nervously accepted the hug and air kisses, giving a halfhearted embrace in return.

"Hello, Diana. You look well." That part was true. Diana had always taken immaculate care of herself, and nothing had changed. In fact, Diana hadn't changed. She looked exactly as Melly remembered her— cool, stylish, and put together. Her clothes were conservative and well-tailored, her hair and makeup flawless, her jewelry expensive and tasteful.

Diana looked up at Kelsey with a curious smile of welcome.

"This is Kelsey Adams," Melly said.

"Melly's boyfriend," Kelsey supplied, oblivious to Melly's dark look. In his mind, it probably wasn't a lie since he refused to take no for an answer.

"How nice," Diana said. She turned once again to Melly, surveying her from head to foot, probably calculating how much Melly's clothes cost. Melly resisted the urge to cross her arms over her midsection as a form of protection. Diana made her feel as if she was standing there naked and vulnerable.

"Have a seat," Diana said, indicating the couch behind them with an imperious wave of her hand. She took the armchair beside them and leaned forward, lacing her fingers together and settling them in her lap. "Well, Melly. Our little Melly all grown up and with a handsome boyfriend, no less." She looked at Kelsey again, assessing him in the same way she had Melly with perhaps a little bit more interest thrown in. Diana was an attractive woman, even if she was older. She would expect Kelsey's look to acknowledge that fact. He gave her his most charming smile and she defrosted slightly.

"What brings you back after so many years away, Melly? We were so sorry when you and Jesus disappeared into thin air. I hope it wasn't something we did." One perfectly sculpted eyebrow arched, and Melly waivered. Was this an invitation to confess, or was she truly curious about what drove Melly away?

"I'm not sure I ever properly thanked you for your kindness back then, Diana. It's not everyone who would take two orphans into her home. I appreciated it." The words felt like a lie, not because Melly hadn't appreciated it, because she had. But she had taken that appreciation and thrown it back in Diana's face. For that she felt horrible. The guilt and shame she had fought for so long returned, settling like bitter acid in her stomach. She had to say something, anything to make it better. "I'm sorry, truly sorry, for the way I behaved back then." The blanket apology wasn't strong enough to garner absolution, but at least Melly had made a stab at making amends.

Diana smiled and gave a dismissive wave of her hand. "Oh, you were a child. Who remembers what happened so long ago?"

An awkward silence descended over the group, which was odd because Diana was a consummate conversationalist, able to talk with anyone about anything. Apparently she wasn't inclined to talk with Melly today, and who could blame her?

"How are the children?" Melly asked. The Tucker's twin daughters —born through a surrogate—had been the light of Melly's young life. She and Jesus had spent many hours playing with them, adoring them. The cynical part of her wondered if that was one of the reasons they had been invited to move in. The kids spent so much time with Melly and Jesus they were rarely with their parents and there was no need to hire a nanny. It had been devastating to leave the two nine year olds without so much as a goodbye.

Diana perked up, the first real emotion on her face since they arrived. "They're doing well." She stood and retrieved a book from the mantle, handing it to Melly. "They're in college this year. Sherry is still trying to find her major, but Shauna is following in Charles' footsteps and majoring in political science."

Melly scanned the photo album with a pang. The twins were identical, but she had no difficulty telling them apart. They were beautiful--blond like their mother with blue eyes like their father. Their clothes were tasteful and, unlike so many kids in their generation, modest. There was no flaunting of skin, no body piercings or tattoos. They looked like two very nice, very well behaved college freshman. Melly smiled as she handed the book back to Diana.

"You must be so proud," she said. "They look like wonderful girls."

"Thank you, they are," Diana said. She not-so-subtly checked her watch. "I'm so sorry to hurry you along, but I have an appointment."

"Of course," Melly said, standing. Kelsey stood, and so did Diana. They faced off and Melly couldn't stop herself from trying again. "Diana, I...I'm sorry. I'm really, really sorry."

It was possible that Diana's face softened slightly, but after so many Botox treatments, it wasn't easy to tell. She studied Melly for a moment, and then seemed to come to a decision. "You weren't the first or the last, Melly. I should have paid better attention and protected you."

Melly blinked at her in surprise for a minute. She shook her head. "That was never your responsibility. I knew better, and I messed up. It's no consolation to you, but I learned and never repeated my mistake."

"It is a consolation, actually." She smiled, but didn't lean forward to offer a hug goodbye. Melly gave her a tremulous smile. Kelsey rested his hand on the small of her back and kept it there as he led her to the car.

"Okay?" he asked once they were in the car.

"Do you think everyone has such a tangible encounter with the sins of their youth?"

"If they did, the world would probably be a better place. There's too little accountability, too much secrecy. Take for example Tucker. If what the ice lady said is true, he's preyed on more girls than you. I would say there are a lot of former interns, secretaries, and maids out there who have his mark on them."

Melly shuddered. What if they had all gotten pregnant? The man might have an army of children he knew nothing about. "Do you think she was the one who sent me the letter?"

"I don't know," Kelsey said. "She's a cool one. Sending the letter seemed like a rash, emotionally-charged thing to do."

"Are we going home now?"

"No, we're going to have fun."

Melly rubbed her temples. She really should have eaten something. "I'm not sure I'm up for fun."

"I know," he said. "But this is phase two. This morning we put everyone in a bag and shook them. Now we see what comes out."

"I don't understand," she said.

"We lit a fuse. Charles will no doubt call in his team for emergency repair work over your appearance. We covered the work front and the home front. Let's hope our mystery mailer feels the threat for what it is and decides to take action."

"You mean you're hoping someone is going to come after us and try to kill me," she clarified.

"It sounds worse when you say it," he said.

"So, where are we going?"

"We're going on our first official date," he said as he made the turn for Balboa Park.

"Do all your dates end in potential murder attempts?" she asked.

"Only the good ones," he said.

"The legend is true: you really know how to show a lady a good time."

"Baby, this is only the beginning," he said. He looked so happy. Melly didn't have the heart to tell him it was nearly the end.

CHAPTER 15

Somehow, Melly was having fun. Maybe because Kelsey was making sure of it. He had always been easy on the eyes, but now he was easy on the heart, too. The first thing they did was get something to eat. Filling her stomach was an automatic mood booster. Kelsey was being very gentle with her, making funny commentary over innocuous subjects he knew would make her laugh without provoking indignation. Usually he delighted in getting a rise out of her. Today he seemed to be delighting in taking care of her, and she was grateful. She wasn't shattered, but she felt more fragile than normal.

After lunch they wandered the gardens, hand in hand. The weather was much warmer than in North Carolina. Melly closed her eyes, allowing Kelsey to lead her as she soaked up the sunshine. They joined a team and played lawn bowling before sitting down to ride the carousel.

When the ride was over, they ate supper. On a normal day, Melly would have teased Kelsey about the bottomless hole in his never-ending hunger. He ate more than three people put together and was almost always thinking about food. But today wasn't a normal day. She trotted behind him, deferring the restaurant selection to him. She picked at her food and shoved it toward Kelsey when she saw him eying it. He finished her food and set their plates aside. Turning toward her, he leaned forward and rested his hands on either side of her in the chair.

"I'm sorry this isn't the date of your dreams, Melly. I know you're ready to go, but I feel like we should give it a little longer."

She clasped her arms on his shoulders because it was the natural thing to do when he was leaning so close. "I'm zonked, but that has nothing to do with you or this date. You're sweet, and I'm having fun."

"Did you call me sweet, Luscious? Because I may need to write this down."

"I would say don't let it give you a big head, but we both know that ship has sailed."

He smiled touching the tip of his nose to hers. "What are you up for next? Lady's choice."

"I saw a band setting up and a flyer for a dance," she said. One of the more enjoyable things about Kelsey being biologically engineered to be a ladies' man was that he liked dancing and was good at it. Dancing was their go-to activity when they couldn't think of anything else.

"Dancing it is," he agreed. "Are you sure you can keep up with me? You've been a bit peckish today. I'm afraid it's made you weak."

"As long as you promise to never say 'peckish' again, then the answer is yes. Also, I've been harboring a secret all these years."

"Yeah? What is it?"

"I spent my adolescent years taking samba lessons. The Latin dances are your Achilles heel. Are you sure you can keep up with me?"

"Bring it on," he said.

She wasn't dressed to dance—no heels or flaring skirt, but she didn't care. She loved to dance. Though she teased Kelsey about not being as good at the Latin scores, he was naturally athletic and took to Samba with his usual grace and enthusiasm.

They were exhausted by the time the Samba band finished playing, but they made no move to leave the dance floor. Instead they stayed for the next set—a jazz trio—and transitioned to slow dancing.

"Want to know a secret, Mel?" Kelsey asked. His arms were at her waist, her hands on his shoulders, making him feel like it was high school prom all over again.

"What's that?" Melly asked. She sounded mellow, or maybe she was simply spent. It had been a long, draining day, and the Samba dancing was strenuous.

"I never liked dancing before I met you," he said.

"Really? But you're so good at it."

"I'm good at everything," he said. "But it wasn't me who was the problem; it was the women. I could never find the right partner. Either they wanted to cling or they wanted to lead. You let me lead, but you do it without being cloying. You hold your own." He wasn't sure he was still talking about dancing because he had described everything that was right between them. Melly was her own person, strong, capable, and independent. She didn't need him to fix her, but she liked it when he tried. He didn't have to prop her up to keep her upright, but she made him want to try, to give of himself, to be there for her. In short, she was perfect for him, and he wondered what took him so long to realize it.

"I think everyone knew about us but us," he blurted as comments their friends made over the years began to make sense.

Melly wanted to kiss him then for his sweetness and transparent vulnerability. No one had warned her love was a razor's edge between pleasure and pain, an odd mix of elation and despair. Kelsey had somehow morphed into everything she wanted in a man, everything except the most important thing. He was laying himself bare for her, and she was going to crush him. She hated that. She wanted to explain, but she didn't want to hurt him, so she did it in Spanish.

"I'm about to break your heart, and you won't understand. You love me because I'm strong and independent, but if I give up what matters most to be with you, I'll cease being me, and you won't love me anymore. *I* won't love me anymore. I never saw myself falling for you, but now that I have, I wonder what took me so long. Thank you for coming with me, for taking care of me, and for being a brother to Jesus. That means more to me than anything else. I wish I could stay right here in San Diego, in your arms, because getting back to the real world is going to ruin everything. You're going to hate me when you finally understand I won't be with you. So, please, remember this moment. Remember I love you."

He smiled down at her, baffled by her flow of words. "You realize I didn't understand a word you said. Except Jesus, something about Jesus."

"That was sort of the point."

"So mysterious, Mellisandra. I'm not used to you speaking Spanish when you're not mad at me. Kind of sexy." He wagged his eyebrows at her, and she laughed.

"I don't always use it when I'm mad at you. I spoke to you when you came to find me at the hotel a few days ago."

"What did you say? It sounded nice."

"I said you were being very sweet, and I liked it."

"I'm always sweet," Kelsey said.

"You know if you lie when you're dancing, it counts double, right?" Melly said.

"You can't make up rules," Kelsey said. He cinched her closer and they danced in silence a few minutes. Kelsey felt an odd sense of impending loss, as if something was slipping away. But she was right here, and he wouldn't let her go anywhere. Maybe it was lingering anxiety. He was better, but he wasn't cured. At least the thought of a few more months of therapy no longer terrified him. He could see the light at the end of the tunnel, and he was anxious to be well again.

The sun was setting, and it was time to go. He was disappointed their game hadn't worked to draw anyone out. Tomorrow they would try again to provoke a reaction, and then they would leave. *And then what?* an uncharacteristically introspective voice tried to intrude, but he wouldn't let it. When they returned home, everything would continue as it was. He and Melly would be together. He would toss his proverbial black book—though, in his case it was an actual black book. He had enjoyed the retro aspect of having a literal black book with hundreds of names in it, sort of his own private joke. But he didn't need it anymore. He and Melly were a done deal. Weren't they?

"We should go," he said, interrupting his melancholy thoughts before they could take root. He wasn't one given to self-doubt, and he saw no need to change that now. Melly was his. The end. Tomorrow would take care of itself, and so would any differences between them. Something would work out; it always did.

It was while they were walking through a darkened section of the park they heard the shot, and this time it wasn't kids shooting at cans. Before Melly's numb brain could process the shock, Kelsey had picked her up and carried her behind a statue. He reached in the waistband of his pants and drew out a Glock. "Use this on anyone who isn't me," he said, handing her the gun. He was secure in the knowledge Lolly had taught her how to use a gun and made her practice until she was adept.

He straightened and took a step away. "Wait a minute," Melly said. "Won't you need this?" She held the gun out to him.

He looked at it and then at her, and a puff of laughter escaped. "Baby, please," he said. "I may be a sniper, but I don't need a gun to hurt someone."

Melly rolled her eyes at his cocky display, but she was smiling as he walked away. Apparently weapons were only necessary for mere mortals, AKA non-marines. But with him went her good cheer and security. She was alone, and somewhere out there was someone who wanted her dead. She crouched against the base of the statue, palming the gun cautiously in her hand. When her brother taught her to shoot, she never envisioned a time the information might come in handy. Never imagined she would be contemplating putting a bullet in another human as she was now.

Right away she knew she wouldn't shoot to kill. She couldn't; it wasn't in her nature. She would aim for a leg or arm, something to slow down her attacker so she could get away. Her breathing became shallow and she rested her head on her knees, nauseated. She was a kindergarten teacher, not a soldier. How had her life come to this? Then she realized she was sitting with her head down, eyes closed—a sitting duck. Her head jerked up in alarm as she scanned the area, but she couldn't see anything, couldn't hear anything over the frantic beating of her heart. How did the guys do this all the time? How did they live in constant fear and danger? No wonder Kelsey was on the verge of a mental breakdown. It was a testament to his mental endurance it had taken this long to happen.

Her backside began to go numb, then her legs, and finally her arms. Still she didn't shift, not wanting to give away her position if someone was watching for her. She thought of something Nick had said once, about how they sometimes had to remain in the same position for days to stake out a target. Melly had a vague idea of what their job entailed, knew it was difficult, but now she was getting a taste of what they had to endure. No wonder Kelsey was cocky. She would be too if she could do what they did. This was torture, and it had only been about a half hour. When she imagined doing it for a lifetime, she wanted to find him and beg his forgiveness for every time she had slighted being a marine, every time she had taken a pin to his too-big head and tried to bring him down to size. From now on, he was allowed to be as cocky as he wanted, at least when it came to his job.

The sound of scraping feet alerted her to someone's presence nearby. She was rational enough to understand she couldn't shoot someone for being near her in a park, but irrational enough to consider everyone a threat. Her hand tensed on the gun. How would she know if she was supposed to use it or not?

"Melly, it's me. I'm coming up on your flank," Kelsey said.

Melly tilted her head against the statue, closing her eyes as a wave of relief washed over her. Kelsey was back; she was safe. "Did you get him?"

"No, but I got her." He came into view, toting a woman in his iron clasp. Melly stood, using the statue to bolster her shaking legs. They stepped into the light, and she gasped.

"Shauna," she said, recognizing the child she used to know from the pictures she had browsed a few hours ago. She was as conservatively dressed as she had been in the photos, a well-tailored pantsuit that looked slightly rumpled with a grass stain on one knee. "Did you tackle her?" Melly asked Kelsey.

"Had to," he replied. "She was trying to kill me."

Shauna looked mutinous as she glared up at him, but when she turned her eyes on Melly, they burned with a feverish hatred. "You ruined my life," she said. "I thought you were so great when I was little, and then I started helping my dad's campaign manager research any skeletons that might have been in his closet. I didn't expect to find anything. Imagine my surprise and disgust when I opened a door and you fell out, you and your baby."

"Shauna, I was a baby myself. I was two years younger than you are now."

"So," Shauna snapped. "I would never be with a married man. I would never tear apart a happy family."

Melly could have told her their situations weren't the same, that Shauna wasn't helpless and alone with a little brother to take care of, that Shauna wasn't being pursued by a man who knew exactly what he was doing, but she didn't want to say any of those things. Not only because she didn't want to bring any more pain, but because she agreed with the younger girl.

"You're right," she said at last. "There was no excuse for what I did. It was horrible. I should have known better, and I'm sorry."

"I don't forgive you," Shauna spat. "I hate you."

Kelsey looked like he was getting ready to open his mouth and jump to Melly's defense. She shook her head to stop him and pulled out her phone.

"Go ahead and call the cops," Shauna said. "You're going to get dragged through the mud along with me."

Melly had already thought of that. She didn't so much care about herself, but some overzealous reporter would no doubt track down Anna and her family and drag them into the debacle. There was also the fact that Melly thought Shauna needed more help than jail would provide. So she called the one person she knew would do whatever it took to make sure Shauna got the sort of help she needed; she called her mother.

If possible, Shauna's outrage became even greater. "Don't involve my mom in this; she doesn't know anything."

Melly tried not to pity her with her glance. *Poor, innocent lamb.* In many ways, she was as untouched as Melly used to be. She knew nothing of the world and thought her father was a saint.

They stood in awkward silence until Diana arrived. Melly began to doubt her decision when Diana swooped in with her usual cool efficiency. Her heels clicked on the flagstone, her steps measured and pronounced. Would she sweep the entire incident under the rug? But when she finally reached them, her eyes were filled with all the concern Melly had hoped to see, and something else she didn't expect—gratitude.

"Thank you, Melly, for not calling the police."

"Mom, don't thank her," Shauna said. She lowered her voice to a whisper. "You don't know what she's like; you don't know what she's done."

"I do, actually," Diana said. She gave her daughter a sad smile. "I know more than you could imagine, Shauna. It's time we had a little talk about your father, something I've been protecting you from all your life, something I hoped you would never find out. But if you're going to be in his world, then you need to know the truth."

Shauna shook her head and took a step back, bumping the statue. "I don't want to know."

"Neither did I," Diana said, sounding cynical and world-weary. She turned to face Melly. "I promise you that you'll never have this problem again. You'll never hear from anyone in my family again, and neither will anyone else connected to you."

"Thank you," Melly said. Shauna was still trying to back away, but Diana captured her, linking her arms in a death grip as she all but dragged her daughter away.

Kelsey came up behind her and placed his hand on her lower back, rubbing out the kinks. "You okay?"

"Yes," Melly said, and was surprised to know she meant it. Anna was safe but, more than that, she had faced the mistakes of her past and realized she had grown from them. She was no longer innocent, but she was also no longer naïve and easily led by her heart. Now she led with her head. She could no longer do whatever she wanted with no regard to the consequences; she had learned her lesson the hard way.

She gazed up a Kelsey with a sad smile. "Let's go home." Her arm slipped around his waist while his arm rested on her shoulders. Side by side, they walked silently to the car.

CHAPTER 16

*J*oan was waiting up on them. Or, more accurately, she was waiting for Kelsey. Melly knew because she only held two chilled beers in her hand.

"Nightcap?" she asked, focused solely on Kelsey as if Melly were invisible.

Kelsey hesitated. Melly knew he was tempted, and not by Joan. After a pregnant pause, he shook his head as if trying to clear it of the image of the beer. "No, thanks, Joan. I've recently given up drinking. Thanks again for keeping us these last couple of days. We're flying out tomorrow. If you're ever in North Carolina, look us up and we'll return the favor." His hand rested on the back of Melly's neck, steering her toward their room. "C'mon, Mel, I'm wiped."

"You've changed," Joan muttered, an aside that probably wasn't meant to be spoken out loud.

I'll say, Melly thought. Not only had Kelsey never been able to refuse a party in a bottle, but he had never been able to refuse flirting with a woman, especially not one as attractive and adoring as Joan.

"You can go first in the bathroom," Melly volunteered. Kelsey was so used to taking military showers he would be in and out in ten minutes. She always had to contend with her hair which somehow added time even when she didn't wash it.

He didn't protest. Instead he gathered his things and left the room. Almost before she could gather her clothes, he was back, smelling like soap and radiating warmth from the shower. She itched to drop her clothes and snuggle up to that warmth and hurried from the room before temptation could overwhelm her.

But when she came back to the room, temptation was lying in her bed. Kelsey lay stretched out on top of the covers, half asleep and taking up all the space. Melly stopped short. "Kelsey," she began, her wary tone rousing him awake.

"I'm not going to sleep here," he said. "I want to hold you for a minute."

"You've probably successfully used that line a million times before," Melly said.

He smiled. "This time I mean it." He held out his arms, but she made no move to step toward them. "C'mon, Melly. We're at a stranger's house and she most likely has her ear pressed to the wall. The last couple of days have been stressful, and someone took a shot at you tonight. I want you in my arms for a few minutes."

He looked and sounded sincere, but Kelsey was a good actor. So it was with some trepidation that Melly made her way to the bed and climbed in, curling in a ball toward him, her hands clasped together at her chest. He mimicked her pose, clasping his hands in front of hers and linking their index fingers.

"Hey," he said, smiling.

"Hey," she replied.

No longer content to clasp her index finger, he let go and took her hand, twining their fingers together. "So, you love me. Let's talk more about that."

"You're never going to let me live it down, are you?" she asked.

"No way. Even if we live to be a hundred and fifty, I'll always remember I won and you said it first. Let me have my moment, Melly; you've been putting me through the paces for three years. Getting you to fall for me was harder than becoming a sniper."

Her amusement fled. "Kelsey, it's not…"

"I know you have this insane idea this isn't the end, that there's some further test I have to pass, but there's not, Melly," he blurted, interrupting whatever she had been about to say.

"Kelsey, it's just that…"

He kissed her, leaning close and pressing his lips to hers in a chaste display of affection that was somehow more disturbing than the few passionate exchanges they'd shared.

The kiss ended and his goal was accomplished; Melly was speechless, at least for a few minutes. "You said you wouldn't," she reminded him.

"I didn't mean to. I'll be good. Don't make me go yet." His fingers smoothed over her lips, caressing. She kept trying to say goodbye, and he didn't want to hear it. They lay in cozy silence a few more minutes while Kelsey's fingers explored the contours of her face. It was relaxing, but he was the first to fall asleep, his palm going slack against her cheek. She reached out to nudge him awake so he could move to the floor, but her hand froze and withdrew. Allowing him to stay was playing with fire, but her brain was tired, her heart sore, and her spirit battered.

Instead of telling him to go, she rolled over, turned off the light, and promptly fell asleep.

In the morning, he had his wish and she was in his arms. She didn't remember cuddling up to him in the night, but apparently she had. Neither wanted to be the first to break the cocoon of intimate silence. They lay motionless except for Kelsey's fingers lightly snaking through her hair. Now was as good a time as any to say what needed to be said. Melly gathered her courage and took a breath.

"Kelsey," she began.

He sat up and swung his legs off the side of the bed. "We should go or we'll miss our flight. Chop, chop, Mel."

Melly's eyes narrowed on his back. He was handling her. She had seen it happen to countless other women he dated. Anytime one of them tried to mention their relationship or a future, he would smoothly change the subject. He was a master, but she never expected it to happen to her.

She hopped out of bed and gathered her things, storming into the bathroom to get ready. When she emerged, he was smiling brightly and chattering like a magpie, which was tactic number two—be so optimistically charming the woman forgets what she wanted to say and can't stay angry. Melly was onto him, though, and she did stay angry, at least for the next few hours.

Somewhere over the middle of the country, her anger dissolved into sadness. Regardless of how he tried to put it off, the outcome was inevitable. Kelsey sensed her mood shift and took her hand, bringing it to his lips for a kiss. She smiled up at him, and his eyes were filled with trepidation lest she might try to talk about them again. She was done trying, though. He already knew how she felt—there was no need to repeat it.

He drove her home. Everyone was at her house, and the sound of laughter echoed from the back patio. The party was probably Ashleigh's doing, not for Melly's sake, but for Caleigh and Travis. After she realized being all but ordered to stay away from each other was making them an irresistible temptation, Ashleigh decided to change tactics. She now thought they should spend as much time as possible together so they would realize how little they had in common. And she also provided safe havens in the form of casual parties to provide them the opportunity to realize they didn't actually like each other. Melly thought it might be working because Travis was starting to pull away.

Melly and Kelsey paused on the front porch, facing each other. "You can't say no, Melly," Kelsey said, dropping her bags and reaching for her. "We would be great, and you know it."

"We would be great, Kelsey, at least in the beginning. Then we would come to the inevitable conclusion we want different things and neither of us is willing to bend. The relationship would end and, with our passionate natures, it would probably end badly. I know you think I'm being a frosty prude or too stubborn and unbending, but I'm trying to preserve what we have now, to save us a whole lot of heartache and pain."

"It's too late for that, Melly, because I am in pain," Kelsey said.

"So am I, but it's the difference between ripping off a bandage and losing an arm."

He picked her up, crushing her to him as he pressed his face to her neck. "Stop being so sensible," he commanded, his voice muffled by her hair. "Lead with your heart, just this once, please."

"No," Melly said, but her voice broke, and she clung to him like a lifeline, a few tears wetting his neck. The tears must have convinced him of her resolve because he slackened his grip and set her down, taking a step back.

"Are you coming in?" she said. "The gang's all here, apparently." She tried to smile, but it wobbled, ruining the effect.

He shook his head, his own smile sad and forced. "For the first time, I think maybe I want to be alone for a while." His hand brushed her cheek, quickly followed by the press of his lips. He lingered, debating with himself about whether or not to kiss her, and then he turned and all but sprinted to his car.

Melly watched him go, dry-eyed and stoic. She gathered her bags and opened the door. Shelby, Ashleigh, and Ashton looked up, which meant Nick must be chaperoning Travis and Caleigh outside.

"Hey, how was the trip?" Shelby said. Her voice was bright and cheerful because she thought Melly was paying a visit to her old home. Ashleigh must not have filled her in on the real reason.

"Good," Melly said. She smiled at the group and began edging toward her room. "I'm wiped out."

"Do you want us to go?" Truck asked. He stood. "I'll get everyone out."

"No," Melly blurted. "Please, you guys stay. At this point, I could sleep even if a marching band decided to practice in my bedroom." She smiled. "I'll catch you all later." She edged down to the bedroom, dropped her bags, and sat on her bed, staring at the floor. She must have left the door open because suddenly Ashleigh was there, a quizzical look on her face.

"Melly, everything okay?"

Melly opened her mouth to reassure her it was, but burst into tears instead. She covered her face and wept. Ashleigh perched beside her and took her in her arms. Melly laid her head on Ashleigh's shoulder and sobbed, not saying a word, allowing Ashleigh to comfort her with soothing words and gentle pats. She didn't remember falling asleep, but somehow she woke the next morning under the covers with her shoes on the floor. Then she glanced at the floor where Kelsey's pallet had been at Joan's house. It was empty, of course. Kelsey wasn't there; Kelsey was gone forever.

Her first instinct was to cry again, but there was work to be done, and life went on. So she mustered her strength, stepped into the shower, and prepared to put one foot in front of the other. Today was a new day, and she would make it through. Eventually it would stop hurting so much, or so she told herself as she stood under the spray and allowed her tears to fall, pretending they were water and she wasn't really crying.

EPILOGUE

For three days, Kelsey stayed away. He had promised to stay in her life, but maybe he was too hurt for that. Maybe she had lost his friendship anyway with her stubborn refusal to give in. The more time passed, the more she doubted her decision to stick to her guns. Maybe he had a point—maybe she was expecting too much. After all, not everyone was guaranteed a happy ending with the person they dated. Maybe she should follow Kelsey's advice and go with the flow for once, forgetting all her talk about marriage and children. Perhaps someday he would be ready for them. Was her time-line so important if it meant not being with him?

She sat on her porch, swinging and musing, when he showed up. He slammed out of his car and her foot stilled the swing. Why did he look so angry?

He bounded the porch steps in one leap and jutted his finger in her face. "Move in with me."

"What?" she asked, sure she had heard him wrong.

"Let's move in together. Technically we'll have to move in here since you own and I rent, plus your house is nicer and doesn't smell like feet, but it loses something to say 'I'm moving in with you,' so I'm asking you to move in with me." He paused waiting for her response and looking for all the world like a little boy who had shoved a bunch of dandelions under his mother's nose, hoping desperately for her approval.

Despite his sweet, anxious-to-please expression, Melly's first reaction was anger. Had he not heard anything she said about marriage and abstinence? But before she could scold him for not listening to her, she reconsidered. This was undoubtedly the biggest move he had ever made in his life. He was beyond terrified, but he was taking a big step. For her, to show her he cared. Misguided as it was, he was making a monumental leap forward. With that in mind, she tried to handle him with kid gloves.

"Thank you for the offer, I love you, but no."

His shoulders sagged. "Why not?"

"Because, Kelsey, it doesn't change anything."

"But I'm committed, Melly. Can't you see that? I thought this would convince you."

She patted the seat beside her and he sat. She rested her hand on his leg. "It's not your commitment I doubt, Kelsey. I guess this is where I tell you it's not you, it's me. I know most other women in the world have no problem with living together or sleeping together before marriage, but I do. I wasn't raised that way, I don't believe that way, and I can't do it."

"Can't you think of it as a compromise? You want marriage, I'm not ready for that. But I'm willing to take the next closest step and live together."

"But what you don't understand is that if I did that I would be compromising *me*."

He ran his fingers through his hair, sighing in frustration. "So, what? You're going to go back to Robert because he meets your criteria?"

"No. I broke up with Robert. It wasn't fair to stay with him once I realized I'll never love him the way he wants me to."

"And now you're going to look for someone else? Because, I have to be honest here, Melly, you're standards are so high I don't think anyone will meet them. Is it better to be alone than to be with me?"

The vulnerability was back, but she was also peeved he was making her seem irrational for sticking to standards that had been in place for millennia until society decided it was too modern for the bonds of matrimony.

"Yes, if it means losing myself in the process of being with you. I would rather be alone with a Melly I like than be with you and not be able to look myself in the mirror."

He crossed his arms over his chest, pouting. "Well, I'm not giving in."

She threw her hands up in frustration. "I'm not asking you to. I'm not trying to trap you or make you come around to my way of thinking. I'm telling you I respect our differences. Why can't you do the same?"

"Because I can't imagine letting you go. I can't imagine living in a world where we're not together, understanding how it could be between us," he said. They sank into heavy silence. He sighed again. "What happens now, between us, I mean?"

"Nothing. We go back to the way it was before—friends."

"And pretend there's nothing between us, pretend we're not dying inside," he said.

"Pretty much," she said.

"I hate this," he said.

"So do I, but I love you, and I'm not willing to give up our friendship to save myself a little bit of emotional torture. Maybe you're a wimp, Marine, but I'm not. I plan to suck it up and hang tough. I'm in this friendship for the long haul."

He laughed and put his arm around her, drawing her close. "Sometimes I hate you, Melly, I really, really do."

She smiled. He used his feet to gently push the swing and the silence was no longer oppressive. Instead it was intimate and comfortable, the kind of silence only two good friends can share. Her phone rang and she pulled away to answer it.

"Hello," she said. The person on the other end of the line spoke, and Melly straightened before bolting upright and covering her mouth with her hand. "Oh, no. I'm so sorry. What can I do? Okay, I will. Love you, and I'll talk to you later." She turned and faced Kelsey, her face ashen. "That was Ashleigh."

He frowned at her shocked, somber tone. "PK? What's up?"

"I need you to go find Nick and restrain him," Melly said.

Now it was Kelsey's turn to bolt out of the swing. "What? Did something happen to Ashleigh? Nick's going to go postal."

"It wasn't anything like that."

"Tell me," he commanded, impatient with the way she was drawing it out.

She took a breath and blurted the news. "Caleigh's pregnant."

THE END? No way. For more of Melly and Kelsey's story, keep reading the fourth and final book in the Brothers Courageous series, *Point Man*. And for more books, please check out my website at www. vanessagraybartal.com